"And it's going to be fun, so prepare yourself." April said the words so softly, he barely heard her.

Something in his chest loosened, and it was easier to flash her a genuine smile. "Are you insinuating I'm not fun?"

She let out a little huff of laughter. "Of course not. Connor Pierce, life of the party."

"Thank you, April." He wanted to say more, to assure her he'd thought this through and it was a good idea. But he hadn't, and as insignificant as a visit to town seemed, the weight of it suddenly crashed over him, making it difficult to catch his breath. He opened the door, the biting cold air a welcome distraction.

Fun was no longer part of his repertoire, so he had five minutes to retrieve parts of himself that he'd shut away after the accident. He'd asked for this, and he had to figure out a way to manage it. It was one afternoon in a small mountain town. How difficult could it be?

CRIMSON, COLORADO:
Finding home—and forever—in the West

D1413171

Dear Reader,

One of my favorite things about writing a multibook series is bringing certain characters into the spotlight. April Sanders was the best friend of the heroine in the first Crimson, Colorado book, and she's made appearances throughout the books as the gentle voice of reason in this quaint mountain town. But her outward calm masks a deep pain, and when she's given custody of two orphaned girls, all of her doubts race to the surface. She has so much love to give but has never expected to be a mother. It will take a Christmas miracle to make her believe she can.

Connor Pierce gave up on miracles—and life in general—the moment his wife and son were killed in a car accident. The reclusive author has come to the remote cabin on Crimson Mountain over the holidays to finish his book. The last thing he wants is to have his life turned upside down by April and her two young charges. But it might be exactly what he needs to mend his heart.

I hope you enjoy the story of these two lost souls who must learn to have faith in each other and the power of love to claim their happy-ever-after.

Merry Christmas!

Michelle

Christmas on Crimson Mountain

—

Michelle Major

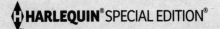
HARLEQUIN® SPECIAL EDITION®

Recycling programs
for this product may
not exist in your area.

ISBN-13: 978-0-373-65099-6

Christmas on Crimson Mountain

Printed in U.S.A.

Michelle Major grew up in Ohio but dreamed of living in the mountains. Soon after graduating with a degree in journalism, she pointed her car west and settled in Colorado. Her life and house are filled with one great husband, two beautiful kids, a few furry pets and several well-behaved reptiles. She's grateful to have found her passion writing stories with happy endings. Michelle loves to hear from her readers at michellemajor.com.

Books by Michelle Major

Harlequin Special Edition

Crimson, Colorado

Always the Best Man
A Baby and a Betrothal
A Very Crimson Christmas
Suddenly a Father
A Second Chance on Crimson Ranch
A Kiss on Crimson Ranch

A Brevia Beginning
Her Accidental Engagement
Still the One

The Fortunes of Texas: All Fortune's Children

Fortune's Special Delivery

The Fortunes of Texas: Cowboy Country

The Taming of Delaney Fortune

Visit the Author Profile page
at Harlequin.com for more titles.

For my fierce and feisty sister-in-law, Jenny.
One of the best perks of marrying your brother
was getting you as friend.

Chapter One

"It's so white."

April Sanders flicked a glance in the rearview mirror as she drove along the winding road up Crimson Mountain.

Her gaze landed on the sullen twelve-year-old girl biting down on her bottom lip as she stared out the SUV's side window.

"It's pretty, right?" April asked hopefully. "Peaceful?" She'd come to love the mountains in winter, especially on days without the sunny skies that made Colorado famous. The muted colors brought a stillness to the forest that seemed to calm something inside of her.

"It's white," Ranie Evans repeated. "White is boring."

"I like snow," Ranie's sister, Shay, offered from her high perch in the booster seat. Shay was almost five, her personality as sunny as Ranie's was sullen.

April didn't blame Ranie for her anger. In the past month, the girls had been at their mother's side as she'd lost her fight with cancer, then spent a week on their aunt's pullout couch before they'd landed in Colorado with April.

Even this wasn't permanent. At least that's what April told herself. The idea of raising these two girls, as their mother's will had stipulated, scared her more than anything she'd faced in life. More than her own battle with breast cancer. More than a humiliating divorce from her famous Hollywood director husband. More than rebuilding a shell of a life in the small mountain town of Crimson, Colorado. More than—

"Can we make a snowman at the cabin?" Shay asked, cutting through April's brooding thoughts.

"You don't want to go outside," Ranie cautioned her sister. "Your fingers will freeze off."

"No one's fingers are freezing off," April said quickly, hearing Shay's tiny gasp of alarm. "You've both got winter gear now, with parkas and mittens." The first stop after picking up the girls at Denver International Airport had been to a nearby sporting-goods store. April had purchased everything they'd need for the next two weeks in the mountains. "Of course we can build a snowman. We can build a whole snow family if you want."

"What we *want* is to go back to California."

April didn't need another check in the rearview mirror. She could feel Ranie glaring at her from the backseat, every ounce of the girl's ill temper focused on April.

"Mom took us to the beach every Christmas. Why wouldn't Aunt Tracy take us to Hawaii with her? Why couldn't you come to Santa Barbara? You used to live in LA. I remember you from when I was little and Mom first got sick."

April tightened her grip on the steering wheel as memories of her friend Jill rushed over her. Taking the turn around one of the two-lane road's steep switchbacks, she punched the accelerator too hard and felt the tires begin to spin as they lost traction.

Ignoring the panicked shrieks from the backseat, she eased off the gas pedal and corrected the steering, relieved to feel the SUV under her control again.

"It's okay," she assured the girls with a forced smile. April was still adjusting to driving during Colorado winters. "The road is icy up here, but we're close to the turnoff for the cabin." She risked another brief look and saw that Ranie had reached across the empty middle seat to take Shay's hand, both girls holding on like the lifeline they were to each other.

It broke April's heart.

She pulled off onto the shoulder after turning up the recently plowed gravel drive that led to Cloud Cabin. The quasi "remote wilderness experience" was an offshoot of Crimson Ranch, the popular guest ranch in the valley, and had opened earlier in the fall. The owners happened to be April's best friend, movie actress Sara Travers, and her husband, Josh. April had first come to Crimson with Sara three years ago, both women burned out and broken down by their lives in Hollywood.

April knew this town could heal someone when they let it. Crimson—and Josh's love—had done that for Sara. April also recognized that she'd held herself back from the community and hadn't truly become a part of it.

Throwing the SUV into Park, she turned to the backseat and met the wary gazes of each of her late friend's precious girls. "I'm sorry your aunt couldn't change her plans for the holidays." She took a deep breath as frustration over Tracy's callous attitude toward her nieces threatened to overtake her. "I'm sorry I couldn't come to California for these weeks. I have a work commitment here that can't be changed."

"I thought you were a yoga teacher." Ranie snatched her fingers away from Shay's grasp. "Who does yoga in the snow?"

"No one I know." April wanted to unstrap her seat belt, crawl into the backseat and gather the surly girl into her arms and try to hug away some of the pain pouring off her. "There's a guest coming to stay at the cabin for Christmas. I need to get there and make sure everything is in order before he arrives. He's a writer and needs to finish a book. He wants the privacy of the mountains to concentrate."

She was already behind, the detour to the airport in Denver pushing back her arrival at Cloud Cabin a few hours. "My job is to cook for him, manage the housekeeping and—"

Ranie offered her best preteen sneer. "Like you're a maid?"

"Like I take care of people," April corrected.

"Like you're taking care of us because Mommy died." Shay's voice was sad but still sweet.

"I am, honey," April whispered around the ball of emotion clogging her throat. She smiled at Ranie, but the girl's eyes narrowed, as if she knew being with April was anything but a sure bet for their future.

April turned up the brightness of her smile as she looked at Shay. "Only about a quarter mile more." She turned to the front and flipped on the radio, tuning it to a satellite station that got reception even in this remote area. "How about some holiday music? Do either of you have a favorite Christmas song?"

"'Rudolph,'" Shay shouted, clapping her hands.

April pulled the SUV back onto the snow-packed road. "How about you, Ranie?"

"I hate Christmas music," the girl muttered, then added, "but not as much as I hate you."

Despite the jab to her heart, April ignored the rude words. She turned up the volume and sang along until the cabin came into view. A driver was bringing Connor Pierce, who was flying into the Aspen airport, to the cabin. The fact that the windows were dark gave her hope that she'd caught at least one break today, and he hadn't arrived before her.

April needed every advantage she could get if she was going to successfully manage these next two weeks.

"No kids."

Connor Pierce growled those two words as soon as the willowy redhead walked into the kitchen.

Maybe he should have waited to speak until she'd spotted him standing in front of the window. Unprepared, she'd jumped into the air, dropping the bag of groceries as she clutched one hand to her chest.

Her wide brown eyes met his across the room, a mix of shock and fear in her gaze. Scaring a woman half to death was a new low for Connor, but he couldn't stop. "They need to go," he snapped, fists clenched at his side. "Now."

To the woman's credit, she recovered faster than he would have expected, placing a hand on the back of a chair as she straightened her shoulders. "Who are you?"

The fact that she didn't scurry away in the face of his anger was also new. Most people he knew would have turned tail already. "What kind of question is that?"

Her eyes narrowed. "The kind I expect you to answer."

"I'm the paying guest," he said slowly, enunciating each word.

"Mr. Pierce?" She swallowed and inclined her head to study him more closely. He didn't care for the examination.

"Connor."

"You don't look like the photo on your website."

"That picture was taken a long time ago." Back when he was overweight and happy and his heart hadn't been ripped out of his chest. When he could close his eyes and not see a car engulfed in flames, not feel his own helplessness like a vise around his lungs.

She didn't question him, although curiosity was a bright light in her eyes. Instead, she smiled. "Welcome to Colorado. I'm sorry you got to the cabin before me." She bent to retrieve the groceries, quickly refilling the cloth bag she'd dropped. "I was told your flight arrived later this afternoon."

The smile threw him, as did her easy manner. "I took an earlier one."

After placing the bag on the counter, she walked forward, her hand held out to him. "I'm April Sanders. I'll be making sure your stay at Cloud Cabin is everything you want it to be."

"I want the kids gone." He didn't take her hand, even though it was rude. She was tall for a woman but still several inches shorter than him. Her long hair was pulled back in a low knot, revealing the smooth, pale skin of her neck above the down coat she wore. The light in her eyes dimmed as her hand dropped.

"I don't know what you mean."

"I saw you come in," he said, hitching a finger toward the window overlooking the front drive. "Are those your daughters?"

She shook her head.

"They can't be here."

"They aren't *here*. They're with me in the smaller cabin next door."

"It doesn't matter." Their voices had drifted up to him when the girls spilled out of the car. The older one, her dark blond hair in a tight braid down her back, had kept her shoulders hunched, arms crossed over her chest as she took in the forest around the house. Connor had felt an unwanted affinity to her. Clearly, she was as reluctant to be trapped in this idyllic winter setting as he was.

It was the younger girl, bright curls bouncing as she pointed at the two log cabins situated next to each other on the property, who had brought unwanted memories to the surface. She'd given a squeal of delight when a rogue chipmunk ran past the front of the SUV. Her high-pitched laugh had raked across Connor's nerves, making him want to claw at his own skin to stop the sensation.

She was dangerous, that innocent girl, threatening his stability on a bone-deep level. "I'm at this cabin to work." He kept his gaze on the window. "I need privacy."

"I'll make sure you have it."

"Not with kids around."

She'd moved so quietly Connor didn't realize April Sanders was standing toe-to-toe with him until he turned back. Up close, with the afternoon light pouring over her, she looked young and too innocent. He'd never seen anything as creamy as her skin, and he had a sudden urge to trace his finger along her cheek and see for himself if it was as soft as it looked.

It was a ridiculous thought. Connor didn't touch people if he could help it. Not for three years, since that drive along the California coast when he'd held his wife's hand for the last time.

Although he knew it to be untrue, he'd come to believe he could hold on to the memory of his wife and son more tightly if he kept himself cut off from physical contact with anyone else. He'd never felt the need before now.

The fact that this woman—a stranger—made him want to change was almost as terrifying as the deadline looming over his head. He took a step back.

"They have no place else to go," she said, the gentle cadence of her voice at odds with the desperate plea he didn't want to see in her eyes. "I promise I'll keep them out of your way."

Connor stepped around her, reaching for the sheet

of paper on the table at the same time he dug in his pocket for his cell phone. "I'm calling Sara Travers."

"No." April snatched the paper with the contact information for Crimson Ranch out of his hand. "You can't." The sheer audacity of the action gave him pause.

"Are you going to hold me here against my will?" He almost laughed at the thought of it, but Connor also hadn't laughed in a longer time than he cared to remember. "I'll call my editor. He'll contact Sara. I assume she's your boss?"

"Please don't." Her voice hitched on the plea, making alarm bells clang in Connor's brain.

"You're not going to cry," he told her. "Tell me you're not going to cry."

She took a breath, blinked several times. "Sara is my boss at the ranch, but she's also my friend. She and Josh just left for a holiday vacation, and I don't want her to worry." April's voice had gone even gentler, almost defeated. Another long-buried emotion grated at his nerves. "She doesn't know about Ranie and Shay yet. If you tell her…"

"She'll make you get rid of them?" he asked, allowing only a hint of triumph to slip into his tone.

"She'll want me to keep them."

He was intrigued despite himself. "Who are those girls to you?" When she only stared at him, Connor placed his cell phone on the table. He couldn't believe he was considering the possibility but he said, "Tell me why I should let them stay."

Chapter Two

April's mind raced as Connor crossed his arms over his chest, biceps bunching under his gray Berkeley T-shirt. He was nowhere near the man she'd expected to be working for the next two weeks at Cloud Cabin.

Connor Pierce was a famous author—not quite on a par with John Grisham, but a worthy successor if you believed the reviews and hype from his first two books. She'd checked his website after Sara had asked her to take on this job as a personal favor.

April had worked full-time at Crimson Ranch when she and Sara had first arrived in Colorado. Although in the past year the yoga classes she taught at the local community center and at a studio between Crimson and nearby Aspen had taken up most of her time, she'd booked off these two weeks. April had been a yoga instructor, as well as a certified nutritionist, to Hollywood starlets and movie actors before her life in California imploded. Apparently Connor Pierce had an extremely stringent and healthy diet, and April felt more comfortable than the ranch's new chef in tailoring her cooking to specific requests.

Based on his publicity photo, Connor was a pudgy, bearded man with a wide grin, so the strict dietary requirements his editor had forwarded hadn't quite made sense. They did for the man in front of her. He was over six feet tall, with dark hair and piercing green eyes in a face that was at once handsome and almost lethal in its sharp angles. As far as she could tell, he was solid muscle from head to toe and about as friendly as a grizzly bear woken from hibernation.

"Ranie and Shay lost their mother last month and their dad has never been in the picture. Jill was an old friend of mine and gave me custody of the girls when she died." She took a deep breath, uncomfortable with sharing something so personal with this seemingly emotionless man. "I can't possibly keep them, but—"

"Why?"

"You ask a lot of questions," she muttered.

He raised one eyebrow in response.

She grabbed the bag of groceries and walked toward the cabinets and refrigerator to put them away as she spoke. "The girls have family in California they should be with on a permanent basis. I'm not a good bet for them." She ignored the trembling in her fingers, forcing herself to keep moving. "They're with me temporarily over the holidays, but I can't send them away. If it's such a problem, we'll go. I'll get you settled, then Sara will find—"

"They can stay."

April paused in the act of putting a bag of carrots into the refrigerator. Connor still stood across the kitchen, arms folded. His green eyes revealed nothing.

"Why?" she couldn't help but ask, closing the refrigerator door and taking two steps toward him. "What made you change your mind?"

"Now who asks too many questions?" He ran a hand through his short hair. "Just keep them quiet and out of my way. I'm over seven months behind on the deadline for my next book. I have until the first of the year to turn in this book before they terminate my contract and…"

"And?"

"I'm here to work," he answered, which wasn't an answer at all. "I need to concentrate."

She nodded, not wanting to push her luck with this enigmatic man. "The food you requested is stocked in the pantry and refrigerator. Cell service is spotty up here, but there are landlines in both cabins. I'll have dinner ready for you at six unless you call. You won't even know we're here with you." Grabbing the empty cloth sack from the counter, she started past him.

He reached for her, the movement so quick it startled her. She stared at the place where his fingers encircled her wrist, warmth seeping through the layers she wore. It was odd because for such a cold man, his touch almost burned.

"I'll know you're here," he said, his voice a rough scrape across her senses. "But keep the girls away from me."

"I will," she promised. Something in his tone told her his demand was more than a need for quiet so he could work.

He released his hold on her a second later and she left, stopping outside as the cold air hit her. She took a couple of breaths to calm her nerves. Yes, she'd have to tell Sara about Ranie and Shay, but not yet. Not until April could find a way to do it without revealing how weak and broken she still was.

And that could take a while.

She hurried across the snow-packed drive, worried that she'd left the girls alone for too long. The cabin was quiet when she entered through the side door.

The caretaker's cabin was much smaller than Cloud Cabin, which had been built to house family reunions and groups of guests who wanted a wilderness experience away from town. In addition to the oversized kitchen, Connor had his choice of five bedrooms, including two master suites, a huge family room and a game room, plus a workout area in the basement. There was a big patio out back with a fire pit and hot tub, but April had a hard time picturing Connor relaxing in the steam and bubbles. It was also better if she didn't try to picture him bare chested because, despite his surly attitude, she'd felt a definite ripple of attraction to Connor Pierce. That was a recipe for disaster.

The girls weren't in the kitchen so she headed upstairs. In this cabin there were only two bedrooms, on either side of the narrow hallway. Sara and Josh had built it to accommodate the small staff needed when there were guests on-site. While construction had been completed in late summer, they'd only taken a few bookings for the fall and hadn't expected anyone to be staying here over the winter months. It wasn't exactly easy to access, although maybe that's what appealed to Connor—or at least to his editor. April knew his debut book had been made into a movie and the sequel was set to release in the spring. She imagined there was a lot of pressure for another blockbuster in the series.

The door to the second bedroom was closed and she had to press her ear to it before she heard voices inside. Both girls looked up when she walked in. "It was so quiet I thought you two might be napping."

Ranie rolled her eyes. "I'm twelve. I don't take naps."

Shay smiled. "I do sometimes, but not today. Mommy used to nap a lot."

April remembered how tired the cancer treatments had made her. All that medicine to make things better, but there were difficult side effects at every stage. "What are you doing?"

Shay held up a tangle of yarn. "I'm finger knitting. I can make you a scarf if you want."

"I'd like that," April said, coming forward to sit on the edge of the other twin bed. "Who taught you to knit?"

"Mommy taught Ranie, and Ranie taught me." Shay pointed to her sister's lap. "She's really good. She can use needles and everything."

April placed her hand lightly on Ranie's knee. "May I see?"

The girl stood up abruptly, shoving what was in her hands into a bag. "I'm not that great. Mostly my rows are crooked. It was just something to do when we sat with Mom."

April tried not to let the girl's constant rejection hurt her, but it was difficult. Ranie looked so much like Jill. "Your mom sent me a sweater one year for Christmas," she told Shay, aware Ranie was listening even as she pretended to ignore them. "I have it with me if you'd like to see."

"Mommy made the best sweaters." Shay tugged her fingers out of the yarn, which to April's eyes looked more like a knot than a scarf. "I mess up a lot."

April reached for the deep red yarn, but Ranie stepped forward and snatched it away. "You're getting better, Shay." She stretched out the jumble until April could see where it almost resembled a scarf. "I'll unknot this and you can keep going."

Shay beamed. "Ranie is the best. She can teach you, too."

"I'd like that."

"Don't you have work to do?" Ranie asked, flipping her long braid over her shoulder. "Taking care of the big-shot author?"

"I'll have time," April told her. "Would either of you like a snack before I start prepping dinner?"

"Can we make the snowman now?" Shay asked, going on her knees to look out the window above the bed.

April thought about the promise she'd made to Connor Pierce. "Because Mr. Pierce is writing a book, he's going to need quiet. I know it's fun to play in the snow, but—"

"I can be real quiet," Shay assured her, not turning from the window. "Ranie and me had to stay quiet when Mommy was sick."

"Ranie and I," April and Ranie corrected at the same time.

When April offered a half smile, Ranie turned away. April sighed. Between the cabin's grumpy houseguest and her own ill-tempered charge, this was going to be the longest two weeks of her life. "Maybe it would be better if we found things to do inside the house."

"He doesn't want us here," Ranie said, her tone filled with righteous accusation. "That's why we have to be quiet. He doesn't want us."

April would have liked to kick Connor Pierce in the shin or another part of his anatomy right now. "He needs to concentrate," she said instead, wanting to make it better for these girls who'd lost so much and were now in a strange state and a strange cabin with a woman who had been their mother's friend but little to them. "It isn't about you two."

"So we can't go out in the snow?" Shay shifted so she was facing April. "We have to stay inside the whole time? That's kind of boring."

Feeling the weight of two different stares, April pressed her fingers to her temples. She should call Sara right now and find someone else for this job, except then she'd have to make holiday plans for these girls. Her work here was a distraction, different enough from real life that she could keep the two separate. It was too much to think of making Ranie and Shay a part of her world. What if they fit? What if she wanted to try for something she knew she couldn't manage?

A remote cabin and its temperamental guest might be a pain, but at least it was safe. Still, she couldn't expect the girls to entertain themselves for two weeks in this small cabin, and neither could Connor.

"Get your snow gear from the shopping bags I left in the front hall," she said after a moment. "As long as we're not making a ton of noise, we can play in the snow as much as you want."

"Mommy liked to rest," Shay said, too much knowledge in her innocent gaze. "Sometimes the medicine gave her headaches, so we know how to be quiet." She wrapped her arms around April for a quick, surprising hug and then scrambled off the bed.

"I'll get your stuff, too," she told Ranie before running from the room. "We're going to build a snowman." April could hear the girl singing as she went down the steps.

Ranie was still glaring at her, so April kept her tone light. "I'd better put on another layer. My sweater and coat are warm but not if we're going to be outside for a while."

"It's me, right?" Ranie's shoulders were a narrow block of tension.

"What's you?"

"The author doesn't want me around," Ranie said, almost as if she was speaking to herself. "It can't be Shay. Everyone loves Shay."

"It isn't about either of you." April risked placing a hand on Ranie's back, surprised when the girl didn't shrug it off. "He's here to work."

"Aunt Tracy bought Shay a new swimsuit," Ranie mumbled, sinking down to the bed.

"For a trip to Colorado in December?"

The girl gripped the hem of her shirt like she might rip it apart. "She wanted to take her to Hawaii with their family."

April shook her head. "No, your aunt told me the trip was only her, your uncle Joe and the boys."

"Tyler and Tommy are annoying," Ranie said.

April smiled a little. "I imagine nine-year-old twin boys can be a handful."

"I guess Aunt Tracy always wanted a little girl,"

Ranie told her, "because I overheard Mom talking to her toward the end. She'd wanted us to live with Tracy, but Tracy would only agree to having Shay." Her voice grew hollow. "She didn't want me."

"Oh, Ranie, no," April whispered, even as the words rang true. Jill's sister had been just the type of woman to be willing to keep one girl and not the other. How could April truly judge when she couldn't commit to either of them?

But she knew the girls had to stay together. "I talked to your aunt before they left on their trip. It's only for the holidays. We have a meeting scheduled with an attorney the first week of January to start the process of transferring custody. She's going to take you both in the New Year. You'll be back in California and—"

"She doesn't want me." Ranie looked miserable. "No one does now that Mom is gone. That author guy is just one more."

"It's not you." The words were out of April's mouth before she could stop them. She hated seeing the girl so sad.

"You're lying." Ranie didn't even pause as she made the accusation and paced to the corner of the room. "Everyone loves Shay."

"Something happened to Connor Pierce that makes it difficult for him to be around young kids."

"What happened?" Ranie stepped forward, hands clenched tightly in front of her. This sweet, hurting girl had been through so much. Once again, April wanted to reach for her but held back. She shouldn't have shared as much as she had about Connor, but she couldn't allow Ranie to believe she was expendable to everyone she met. At least this way, Ranie could help shield Shay, keep her out of Connor's line of sight.

April met Ranie's clear blue gaze. "His wife and son died in a car accident a few years ago. The little boy was five at the time."

"Shay's age," Ranie whispered. The girl's eyes widened a fraction.

Good. The news was enough of a shock on its own. April didn't have to share anything more. Not the images she'd seen online of the charred shell of a car after the accident and fire that had killed Connor's family. Not the news report that said he'd also been in the vehicle at the time of the crash but had been thrown clear.

She hoped he'd been knocked unconscious. The alternative was that Connor Pierce had watched his family die.

Connor glanced at the clock on his phone again, staring at the bright numbers on the screen, willing them to change. When they did and the numbers read 6:00 on the dot, he jumped out of the chair in front of the desk, stalked toward the door, then back again.

He knew April was in the kitchen, had heard her come in thirty minutes ago. He'd been staring at the clock ever since. Minutes when he should have been working, but the screen on his laptop remained empty.

Every part of his life remained empty.

When his editor had suggested taking two weeks at a remote cabin to "finish" his manuscript, Connor hadn't argued. He hadn't wanted to explain that he still had over half the story to write. It had even made sense that a change of scenery might help him focus.

That's how it worked with writers, right? A quiet

cabin in the woods, an idyllic setting to get the creativity flowing. What Connor understood, but wouldn't admit, was that his inability to write came from the place inside him that was broken. There was simply nothing left, only a yawning cavern of guilt, regret and sorrow. Emotions he couldn't force himself to mine for words to fill a manuscript, even one that was seven months past due.

He shut the laptop and headed downstairs, the scent coming from the kitchen drawing him forward. That was as unexpected as everything else about April Sanders, since food was no longer something from which Connor derived pleasure. He ate for energy, health and to keep his body moving. He didn't register flavor or cravings and lived on a steady diet of nutrition bars and high-protein meals that were bland and boring.

Nothing about April was bland or boring, a realization that fisted in his gut as she turned from the stove when he walked into the room.

"How's the writing going?" she asked with a smile, as if they were friends. She wore a long-sleeved shirt that revealed the curve of her breasts and waist, with a pair of black yoga pants that hugged her hips. April was slim, with the natural grace of a dancer—someone aware of her body and what it could do. Her hair was still pulled back, but the pieces that had escaped to frame her face were curlier than before.

"I could hear the kids playing outside," Connor said, and watched her smile fade. This was who he was now, a man who could suck the warmth out of a room faster than an arctic wind.

"We stayed on the far side of the caretaker's cabin

and the girls weren't loud," she answered, pulling a plate from a cabinet.

"I still heard them."

She glanced over her shoulder. "Were you pressing your ear to the window?"

He opened his mouth, then shut it again. Not his ear, but he'd held his fingertips to the glass until they burned from the cold. The noise had been faint, drifting up to him only as he'd strained to listen. "Why were they outside? It's freezing up here."

"Shay wanted to play in the snow." April pulled a baking tray out of the oven and set it on the stove top. "They're from California so all this snow is new for them."

"Join the club," he muttered, snapping to attention when she grabbed a foil-wrapped packet on the tray and bit out a curse.

She shook out her fingers, then reached for a pair of tongs with her uninjured hand.

He moved closer. "You need to run your fingers under cold water."

"I'm fine," she said, but bit down on her lower lip. "Have a seat and dinner will be—"

He flipped on the faucet as he came to stand next to her. Before he could think about what he was doing, Connor grabbed her wrist and tugged her the few feet to stand in front of the sink. He couldn't seem to stop touching this woman. He pushed up her sleeve and positioned her hand under the cold water from the faucet. "If the burn is bad enough, it will blister your fingertip."

"I wasn't thinking, but I'm not hurt," she said softly, not pulling away.

She was soft against him, the warmth of her both captivating and an irritation against the shell he'd wrapped around himself. She smelled subtly of lavender, and Connor could imagine April standing in a field of it in the south of France, her red hair a beautiful contrast to the muted purple of the plants. Fanciful thoughts for a man who'd become rigid in his hold on reality.

"It's better to be safe."

He didn't want to examine why he kept his grasp on her wrist and why she didn't pull away. She wasn't going to blister—the burn from the foil was a surface injury at most. That meant... He met her gaze, gentle and understanding, then jerked away as if he'd been the one scalded by the heat.

"What do you know about me?" he asked through gritted teeth.

She took a moment to answer, turned off the tap and dried her hand before looking up to him. "Only what I've read in old news reports."

Gripping his fingers on the edge of the granite counter, he forced himself to ask, "And what did they tell you?" He'd purposely not read any of the press after the crash.

"Your wife and son were with you during the promotional tour for your last book release three years ago. There was a car accident on the way to an event— another driver crossed the median and hit you head on—they were both killed."

"We all should have died in that wreck," he whispered.

"You were thrown from the car. It saved your life."

She didn't dispute his observation, which he appreciated. Part of why he'd initially cut so many people out of his life after the accident was that he couldn't stand hearing any more theories about why he'd lived while Margo and Emmett had died. That it was fate, a greater plan, some universal knowing to which he wasn't yet privy.

Connor knew it was all nonsense. If there had been any sense in the tragedy, it would have been for him to perish while his beautiful wife and innocent son survived. Anything else was blasphemy as far as he was concerned.

"Unfortunately, it did," he agreed, wanting to shock her. He'd spent hours wishing and praying for his own death in the months after the accident. His whole reason for living had been stolen from him, and he hadn't been strong enough to save either his wife or son. He'd wallowed in grief until it had consumed him. The pain had become a part of his makeup—like another limb or vital organ—and it pushed away everyone and everything that didn't make it stronger.

Eventually, the grief had threatened to destroy him, and Connor had shut it down, his will to live stronger than his wish to die. But in excising the pain, he'd had to cut out other parts of himself—his heart, the connections he had to anyone else in the world who he might fail with his weakness. Perhaps even his creativity. The ability to weave stories was so much a part of him that he'd taken the gift for granted. Except, now it was gone, and he had no idea how to get it back.

The feel of April brushing past pulled him from his thoughts. She placed a plate of food on the table at the one place setting and bent to light the candle that sat in the center of the table.

"That's not necessary," he told her, his voice gruff.

"I light candles for all the guests." She straightened. "Would you like wine with your meal?"

"Water, but you don't have to serve me."

"Actually, I do," she said with a wry half smile. "It's my job, and I'm good at it."

"Why aren't you asking me questions about the accident?"

She studied him for a moment, a hint of pink coloring her cheeks. "Do you want to talk about it?"

He shook his head.

"That's why," she said simply, and walked back to the kitchen to fill a glass from the water dispenser in the refrigerator.

The fact that she wasn't pushing him made Connor want to tell her more. As soon as people started asking questions, whether it was his editor, the therapist his publisher had hired, or one of his sisters or his mother, Connor shut down.

Yet the need to share details of the nightmare that had defined his recent life with April was almost overwhelming in its intensity. His chest constricted, an aching reminder of why he kept silent. To talk about Margo and Emmett was to invite pain and sorrow back into his life. Connor couldn't do that and continue to function.

"I'm going to check on the girls," she told him after placing the water on the table. "I'll be back in a few minutes—"

"What if I want you to stay while I eat?"

She paused, meeting his gaze with those big melty chocolate eyes. There was something in them he didn't understand, not pity or wariness as he would have expected. It looked almost like desire, which he couldn't fathom. He had nothing to offer a woman like April, someone so full of light and peace. The darkness inside him would blot her out, muting her radiance until she was nothing. That's how the darkness worked, he'd realized, and there was little he could do to stop it.

"Then I'll stay," she said.

He let a sneer curl his upper lip. "Because it's your job?"

She didn't blink or look away. "Because you asked me."

A lightning-quick bolt of emotion passed through him, forcing him to take a step back when all he wanted to do was move closer to her. The unfamiliarity of that urge was enough to have him piling the silverware and napkin on the plate, then picking it up along with the glass. "I'm going to eat in my room. I have work to do on an important scene for the book."

"You can leave your plate outside the bedroom door," she said in that same gentle voice. What would it take to rattle a woman like April? "I'll clean it when I get back."

"Fine," he said, purposely not thanking her or acknowledging the effort she'd put into the meal that smelled better than anything he'd eaten in ages. His rudeness was another shield, and he'd need as many as he could create to resist the things April made him feel.

Chapter Three

April let herself into the main cabin before sunrise the next morning. The girls were still sleeping and, before leaving the caretaker's cabin, she'd prepared a pan of cinnamon rolls to bake when she returned. She needed to make breakfast for her cantankerous guest but didn't want to take the chance of seeing Connor again so soon. The previous night had jumbled her nerves in a way she barely recognized.

Connor Pierce was arrogant, ill-mannered and a borderline bully. But the pain she'd seen in his eyes when he spoke of the accident that had claimed his wife and son touched her at a soul-deep level. Just as his actual touch made her skin heat with need. Her reaction was inappropriate at best and, more likely, damaging to a heart she'd learned the hard way to protect and guard.

Thankfully, he hadn't reappeared last night when

she'd returned to clean the kitchen. His empty plate had been left on the counter, the cabin quiet as she'd put everything away. A light had still burned in the upstairs window when she'd walked across the dark night to her cabin but that had been the only indication Connor was still awake.

April was grateful since she wasn't sure she would have been able to resist questioning him more on the heartbreak of losing his family. There was no doubt the grief had been substantial, and she could use advice on how to guide Ranie and Shay through the sorrow of losing someone they loved, even if the circumstances were totally different. April had thought she understood heartbreak after her divorce but later realized that the scars from Daniel leaving had more to do with rejection and humiliation than love.

She started coffee, preheated the oven and then unpacked the lidded container she'd prepped at the other cabin. There was a nonstick muffin tin in the drawer next to the oven, and she began to dump egg-white-and-vegetable mix into the openings. Each move she made was quiet and purposeful so as not to make noise. Her goal was to get everything ready, then leave before Connor woke.

"You're up early."

April jumped at the sound of that gravelly voice behind her, the mixture sloshing over the side of the glass bowl. "Is your goal to give me a heart attack?" She set the bowl on the counter and grabbed a wad of paper towels to clean up the mess.

"You spook easily," he told her. "It's the only time you raise your voice."

"You shouldn't sneak up on people. It's rude." Tossing the paper towels into the trash can under the sink, April turned, planning to enlighten Connor Pierce on what she sounded like when shock turned to anger. The words caught in her throat at the sight of him standing on the far side of the island wearing only a pair of loose gym shorts, his chest broad and hard and glistening with sweat.

Glistening. Oh, my.

"There's a workout room downstairs," he said, wiping a small white towel across his face and down his front. April followed the movement, the muscles and smattering of hair across his chest making her mouth go dry. She'd thought herself immune to men and the heavy pull of attraction since her divorce. Many of her girlfriends in Crimson were involved with handsome men, but April had never noticed any of them other than with the affection reserved for brothers.

What she felt for Connor was different and dangerous.

Instead of berating him more for startling her, she asked, "Do you need anything?" and hated that she sounded breathless.

"A shower."

Spoken in his deep voice, those two words sounded like an invitation. April felt her cheeks color. She grabbed the muffin tin and shoved it into the oven, hoping the heat that wafted out would provide a decent excuse for her blush. "I can have breakfast ready in about twenty minutes. Are you always up at this time?"

"I don't sleep much."

"Too inspired?"

She'd been referring to his writing, but one side of his mouth kicked up like he'd taken the question another way. "Not yet," he answered. "But there's time for that."

She didn't understand his mood this morning. He was relaxed and almost flirty, different from the tense, bitter man she'd encountered yesterday.

"Working out helps me," he offered, as if reading her mind. "Gives me an outlet that I find calming."

"I teach yoga," she said with a nod. She opened the dishwasher and started putting away the clean dishes. "It does the same thing."

"Do you teach at Crimson Ranch?" He moved closer, took a seat at the island. Connor seemed unaware of the effect his upper body was having on her, and she tried to ignore her reaction. Even if he hadn't been a guest, this man was not for her.

She filled a glass with water and placed it on the counter in front of him. "During the summer months, I teach at the ranch. There's also a community center in town that offers classes, and another studio between Crimson and Aspen."

"You've done yoga for a while?" he asked, taking a long drink. A droplet of water traced a path along his strong jaw, then over his throat and down the hard planes of his chest. He wiped it away, then met her gaze. It took April several seconds to realize he was waiting for an answer to his question.

"Almost fifteen years." She concentrated on unloading the dishwasher as she spoke. "I had some injuries from dancing when I was younger, and yoga helped my body heal. I owned a studio in California for a while." She'd loved the studio she'd built from the ground up, but it had become one more casualty of her illness and then the divorce.

"But you teach for other people here?"

April felt her eyes narrow. Connor was a little too insightful. The woman who owned the private studio outside of town had offered to sell the business to April on several occasions. Marty was in her seventies, ready to retire and move closer to her adult children and their families, but she felt a loyalty to the local clients she had in the area. April knew the older woman had received offers from at least two national chains, but Marty hoped her studio would remain locally owned.

"It gives me more flexibility," she answered.

"Do you travel?"

She focused her attention on the basket of knives and forks. "No."

"Have a big family?"

She shook her head, not liking where this line of questioning was leading.

"Why is flexibility important?"

How was she supposed to explain? It was the answer she always gave, and no one had ever questioned her answer. Not until Connor.

April loved Colorado and the town of Crimson, but as much as she was grateful for a new start and the friends that were part of it, there was something missing. A broken piece inside that prevented her from truly committing to this town the way Sara and so many of their friends had in the past couple of years.

There was too much at stake for April, because if she devoted herself to making a life here the way she had in California and then lost it again, she wasn't sure she'd survive. It was easier to play the part of caretaker and helpful friend. Those roles allowed her to be a part of the community without investing the deepest pieces of her heart and soul in anyone.

Giving too much—feeling too much—left her vulnerable to pain, and she'd had enough pain to last a lifetime.

"Why do you care?" she asked, slamming the empty silverware basket back into the dishwasher and closing the machine's door. She hated how this man riled her but couldn't stop her reaction to him any more than she could deny the attraction she felt. All she could do was ignore them both.

He pushed the empty glass across the counter. "Just making conversation," he said as he stood, his gaze steady on hers. There was a teasing light in his eye, and awareness danced across her skin in response. He didn't seem upset by her rudeness or realize how out of character it was. But *she* knew and it scared her. "We're the only two people here so—"

"Actually, we're not." She placed her palms down on the cool granite and leaned toward him. "There are two sweet, sad girls in the other cabin who are afraid to make a sound in case they get me in trouble."

"They don't belong here," he said, the warmth in his voice disappearing instantly.

"They don't belong anywhere," she countered. "That fact doesn't make it easier to manage. I'd think you would understand—"

"I'm here to work." He pushed away from the island. "Not to play grief counselor."

"How's the writing going? Is being alone in this cabin inspiring you?"

She thought he'd walk away so was surprised at his quiet answer. "I'm always alone."

Just when she'd worked up a good temper, one that could hold her attraction at bay, he'd done it again. Let a bit of vulnerability slip through the impenetrable shields he had to curl around her senses.

April understood *alone*. She knew the emptiness of loneliness but also the safety it provided. She didn't want to have that in common with Connor, because it was a truth she hadn't shared with anyone else in her life. If he recognized it in her...

"You don't have to be," she said quietly, and the words were as much for her as him. She wanted to believe them even as the fear that lived inside her fought against it.

"Yes, I do." He ran a hand through his hair, the damp ends tousling. "I'm going to take that shower."

"Breakfast will be ready when you're finished. I'll—"

"Leave it," he snapped. "I don't need you to wait on me."

She opened her mouth to protest, but he held up a hand. "Don't worry. I won't complain to anyone. It's distracting to have you in and out. Leave the food and I'll take care of myself. I'm used to it."

He didn't wait for an answer before stalking from the kitchen.

April blew out an unsteady breath. She was making a mess of this. Sara still had ties to Hollywood and continued to act when the right roles came along. Not as much since expanding the ranch, but the studio that held the movie rights to Connor's books was important to Sara. It's why her friend had agreed to arrange two weeks at the cabin for him. It was also why Sara had asked April to step in and help. April's talent was

caring for people. It was something she enjoyed and a
gift she used both at the ranch and while teaching her
yoga classes. She normally had an easy way with even
the most demanding guests.

But she was at her worst with Connor, and she hated
it. As abrasive as he could be, he was also her client,
and he'd survived a life-altering tragedy that should
make her more sympathetic to him.

She imagined that Connor hated sympathy—she
had during her battle with breast cancer. The pitying
looks and fake support from the women she'd thought
were her friends had added an extra layer of pain to her
life. Those so-called friends had said the right things
but quickly distanced themselves when the treatments
robbed her of strength, her looks and most of her dignity. Only Sara had remained at her side, driving her to
and from appointments and helping her to move when
Daniel had filed for divorce in the middle of her second round of chemo.

The oven beeped, drawing her from her thoughts.
She removed the egg muffins and placed them on a
rack to cool. Pulling a plate from the cabinet, she set
the table, poured a small glass of juice, then set a bowl
of cut melon next to the plate. Connor may not need
someone to look after him, but that was April's job
here. She was going to take care of that man whether
he liked it or not.

Hand lifted in front of the heavy oak door, Connor
drew in a breath, the cold air making his lungs burn.
He welcomed the sharp stab of pain because physical
pain helped him remember he was still alive. It was
part of the reason he worked out so compulsively—

pushing his body to the point of exhaustion gave him a sense of connection to something. Also, Connor had vowed never to be weak again. His weakness was the reason Margo and Emmett had died.

What he was about to do was madness, but he knocked on the door anyway.

It took only a moment for it to open, and he was looking down at a young girl with angelic blond curls, huge blue eyes and a smudge of something across her cheek. The impulse to wipe his thumb across her face was a punch to the heart. He almost turned and ran, even though that would mark him as the coward he was. Emmett had always had a smear or stain on some part of him. His son's favorite food had been peanut-butter-and-jelly sandwiches, and there was normally a telltale spot of grape jelly on the corner of his mouth and sticky fingers, leaving marks on everything the boy touched.

Connor had often balanced writing with parenting duties if Margo had an appointment or meeting. His preoccupation with his work had sometimes left Emmett, even at five, to slap together sloppy sandwiches for both of them. Emmett loved being in charge, and Connor had been happy to have something to eat that he didn't have to make. After the accident, he'd spent hours wishing he could have a daddy do-over. He would have put aside his precious words to take care of his more precious son.

"Are you a delivery man?" the girl asked when he stared at her.

He shook his head, not yet trusting his voice when memories threatened to pull him under like a riptide.

"Mommy said Santa Claus uses real delivery people to help bring toys at Christmas so they don't feel left out because he's got a sleigh and they don't. Last year Santa had the delivery man bring me three sparkly ponies and a new set of markers." She wiped the back of her hand across her nose. "Do you like to draw?"

"I like to write," he answered automatically. "At least I used to."

She nodded. "I'm good at writing. My teacher said my big *G* is perfect."

"Shay, shut the door." Another voice drifted forward. "It's freezing."

A moment later, a different girl appeared behind the little one. They were clearly sisters, although the older girl's hair was a darker blond and her eyes a deeper blue. "Who are you?" She placed a hand on her sister's shoulder.

"He likes to write, Ranie," Shay announced. "But he's not helping Santa."

"I need to talk to April," he told Ranie.

"She's getting ready to take us to town," Shay answered before her sister could speak, "to buy games to help us be quiet. The man who lives next door hates kids." She bounced on her small feet. "We're going to see the lights and get hot chocolate."

"I don't hate kids," Connor muttered, shifting under Ranie's gaze. He was certain the girl knew exactly who he was.

"That's good," Shay told him. "You should stay away from the other man. He might not like grown-ups either."

"No doubt," he heard Ranie mumble.

Instead of making him angry, Connor had the strange

urge to smile. He liked this girl standing sentry, still holding on to her sister as she tried to fill the doorway with her small frame. "Where's April?"

"I'll get her." Ranie went to close the door in his face, but Shay stepped forward.

"We have to invite him in," Shay said, grabbing his hand and tugging him forward before he could react. "He's nice."

He fought the need to jerk away from her small hand and allowed himself to be led into the smaller cabin.

"Shay, you don't know that he's nice. This man—"

"What's going on?"

As the door clicked shut behind him, he looked up to see April silhouetted by the late-morning light. She wore a pair of dark jeans and knee-high boots with a thick gray sweater. It was the first time he'd seen her hair down, the gentle red curls falling over her shoulders.

Shay didn't let go of his hand, and Connor could feel the imprint of her soft skin like a brand. The pain was fierce, radiating up his arm and through his chest to the empty place where his heart used to be.

"You left your phone at the other cabin." He pulled the device from his coat pocket with his free hand and held it out.

"I could have taken it at the door." Ranie reached forward and pulled Shay away from him. "You don't hold hands with a stranger," she scolded.

"He's not a stranger." Shay pushed a curl off her forehead. "He's April's friend. He had her phone." She glanced up at him. "Right?"

April took the phone from his hand, her cool fingers

brushing his palm. "Mr. Pierce is staying next door at the cabin," she told Shay, ruffling the girl's hair. "He's busy working, so it was nice of him to bring the phone to me."

Shay glanced between April and Connor, her mouth dropping open. "But the man living next door hates kids. You don't hate me, do you?" she asked him, her blue eyes wide with disbelief.

"Shay, shut up," Ranie said on a hiss of breath.

April threw Connor an apologetic look. "I never said—"

"I don't hate you," he told the little girl.

She pointed to her sister. "See, he's nice and my friend and April's friend and you shouldn't say 'shut up.' Mommy didn't like it."

"Mom isn't here." Ranie glared at Shay. "She's—"

"Enough." April's tone was firm. "You girls go get your coats, hats and mittens and we'll head to town."

Ranie stalked off down the hall, but Shay continued to stand next to him, her chin quivering the tiniest bit. "Do you want to go to town with us and get hot chocolate?"

He started to shake his head when she added, "Because I know you're nice even if Ranie doesn't think so. She gets extra grumpy because our mommy died, and that makes her act mean. But she's really just sad inside."

The wisdom in those words leveled him. Connor had been used to being angry since the accident. He had cut people out of his life and pushed them away with his moods until the rage inside him felt like all that was left. What if he had held on to the anger so he didn't have to feel the lingering sorrow of loss?

"Will you go?" Shay asked again when he didn't respond. "It's a long way down the mountain, so April said this trip is special."

"Shay," April said quietly, "that's nice of you to offer, but Mr. Pierce has—"

"I'll go."

The girl smiled and clapped her hands. "I knew we were friends. I'm going to go get my winter coat. April bought it for me new because in California we don't have snow. You should wear gloves and a hat because there's an ice-skating rink in the park downtown and if it's not too crowded we can try it."

Connor watched her run down the hall and disappear around a corner before he met April's dubious gaze. "Does she always talk that much?"

She gave a small nod. "Shay talks and Ranie sulks. Why did you tell her you'd come to town with us?"

"Because she asked me," he responded, echoing her words from last night.

Her eyes widened a fraction, but she didn't acknowledge the repetition. "What about writing?"

He shrugged. "I need a break."

"What about needing the girls to be quiet?" she asked, her mouth thinning. "I'm not going to demand they don't talk."

He wanted to press the pad of his thumb to her full lower lip. This need to touch her, to be near her, was a slippery slope that could only lead to complications for both of them. It had driven him across the property when he should be working. Now the thought of April and the girls leaving him totally alone up here on the mountain had him agreeing to a jaunt into town when he hadn't allowed himself to be social or out in public for years. He was used to being alone, had meticulously carved out the solitary existence he lived. But he couldn't force himself to turn around.

"I realize that was an unfair request." He tried to offer a reassuring smile, but his facial muscles felt stiff from underuse. "I'd like a do-over. Please."

Part of him hoped she'd refuse and he could crawl back into the reclusive hole that had become his life. At least there he was safe. A deeper piece of him needed the companionship and acceptance April could provide. As much time as he spent alone in his apartment in San Francisco, he thought he might go crazy if left by himself on Crimson Mountain. He couldn't let—

"We'll leave in five minutes." April said the words so softly he barely heard her. "And it's going to be fun, so prepare yourself."

Something in his chest loosened and it was easier to flash her a genuine smile. "Are you insinuating I'm not fun?"

She let out a little huff of laughter. "Of course not. Connor Pierce, life of the party."

"That's me."

"Grab your stuff, Mr. Party Pants." She held his gaze for several long moments, then shook her head. "This should be interesting."

"Thank you, April." He wanted to say more, to assure her he'd thought this through and it was a good idea. But he hadn't and, as insignificant as a visit to town seemed, the weight of it suddenly crashed over him, making it difficult to catch his breath. He opened the door, the biting-cold air a welcome distraction.

Fun was no longer part of his repertoire, so he had five minutes to retrieve parts of himself that he'd shut away after the accident. He'd asked for this, and he had to figure out a way to manage it. It was one afternoon in a small mountain town. How difficult could it be?

Chapter Four

As it turned out, April could have promised silence to Connor on the way into town. Neither of the girls spoke as they made the slow drive down the curving mountain road. Glancing in the rearview mirror, April saw that Ranie kept her gaze firmly out the window, although the girl seemed lost in her thoughts rather than intent on the view. Shay couldn't seem to take her eyes off Connor, who was sitting still as a statue next to April. The little girl was studying him as if he was a puzzle with a missing piece.

Two missing pieces, she thought. She'd endured losses in life but couldn't imagine the pain he must have felt losing his wife and son. The need to comfort and care for him crawled up her spine, coming to rest at the base of her neck, uncomfortable and prickly like an itch she couldn't quite reach. That inclination in her was her greatest strength and biggest weakness, but mixed with her body's reaction to Connor, it was downright insanity.

Sara was forever trying to find a man for April. It had become her friend's singular mission to see April happy and in love. April had gone on dates with a few nice men, but ended things before they got remotely serious.

She'd been in love once, thought she and her ex-husband had been happy, but understood now that was only an illusion. When her marriage had ended, she'd vowed never to make herself vulnerable to anyone again. She'd convinced herself she was content on her own. It had been easy enough to believe, especially since she hadn't felt the heavy pull of physical desire for a man since her divorce.

Until a rushing awareness of the man next to her had buried all of her hard-won peace in an avalanche of need and longing she could barely process.

As if sensing the thread of her tangled thoughts, Connor shot her a glance out of the corner of his eyes. Barely a flicker of movement, but she felt it like an invisible rope tugging her closer. His gaze went back to the road after a second, and she noticed his knuckles were white where his fingers gripped his dark cargo pants. He was nervous, she realized, and somehow that chink in his thick, angry armor helped her regain her composure.

There was so much sorrow and loss swirling through this car, and it was up to her to ease the pain. Christmas was a time for joy and hope, and she was going to give a little bit of it to these three people under her care.

"I forgot to turn on the radio," she said, making her voice light.

Ranie groaned from the backseat. "Not more corny holiday music."

April flipped on the radio and the SUV's interior was filled with a voice singing about grandma and a reindeer. "That's called karma," April told the girl with a laugh. "You said 'corny' and that's what we've got." She sang along with the silly song for a couple of bars and felt her mood lighten. Maybe it was so many winter breaks spent working retail during high school and college, but holiday music always made her feel festive.

"Santa and his reindeer fly," Shay said brightly as the song ended. "Why would the grandma get run over if she was walking?"

"Kid has a point," Connor muttered.

April smiled at his grouchiness because at least he was talking and he'd loosened his death grip on his pant legs. "Maybe it was when Santa's sleigh was taking off after delivering presents," she told Shay, "so he was still on the ground."

"But shouldn't he take off from the roof?" Shay asked.

She glanced at Connor for help. He arched his brow and didn't say anything.

April turned off the mountain road onto the two-lane highway that led toward downtown Crimson. She met Ranie's gaze in the rearview mirror as she pulled up to a stop sign at the bottom of the hill.

The girl rolled her eyes, then looked at her sister. "Maybe they didn't have a chimney at their house," she said, her tone gentler than April would have expected from the sullen tween. "And Santa was parked in the backyard. Remember how Mom told you he's magic? That's how he can deliver all the toys and find kids even if they're visiting family for Christmas."

"So even though we're not with Aunt Tracy in Hawaii, he'll know to find us in Colorado?"

Ranie nodded. "Yep. Besides, it's just a song, Shay. Santa wouldn't really run over someone's grandma."

"Thanks, Ranie." The young girl reached over and took her sister's hand. April saw Ranie's eyes close as her chest rose and fell with a breath so weighty it was a wonder the girl's shoulders didn't cave under it. April wanted to cry for the unfairness of a twelve-year-old who was her sister's emotional anchor.

Tears wouldn't help these girls. But holiday spirit might. She turned up the volume for a classic remake of "Baby, It's Cold Outside" and sang the part that Margaret Whiting had made famous. "Want to be the man?" she asked, glancing at Connor as she eased onto the exit for downtown.

"I *am* a man," he answered, his tone grumbly.

"She meant in the song, silly," Shay called from the backseat.

"I don't know the words."

"April knows the words to all the Christmas songs," Shay said.

"It's like a curse," Ranie added.

One side of his mouth curved.

"What's your favorite holiday song, Connor?" April asked, slowing the car as they hit the steady stream of traffic that bottlenecked Crimson's main street throughout the winter ski season.

He gave her a look like she'd just asked whether he wanted his hands or feet cut off first.

"Everyone has a favorite song," she insisted. "Shay's is 'Rudolph the Red-Nosed Reindeer' and Ranie's is..." She paused, holding her breath.

"'Silent Night,'" the girl said on an annoyed huff of breath.

April didn't bother to hide her smile. "Give it up, Connor. I'm guessing you're not the 'Rocking Around the Christmas Tree' type. If I had to pick—"

"'O Holy Night,'" he told her.

"Nice choice," she said with a smile then turned her attention back to the road. She found a parking space a couple of blocks off Main Street. The snow was packed down on the roads, but the sidewalks had been cleared. "The lighting of the big tree in the town square was last week, so we missed that," she said as Connor and the girls got out of the car. "But the stores are all decorated so it's fun to shop and—"

"It's never fun to shop," Connor said, glancing around at the historic buildings and painted Victorian storefronts that made up downtown Crimson. "This place looks like a movie set."

April smiled. "It's beautiful, right?"

"It looks fake," he corrected.

She started to narrow her eyes, then forced an even brighter smile on her face. "The best part about Crimson is that it's not fake. This is a real town filled with people who love the holidays. It's a wonderful place to live."

Shay returned her smile. "I like it."

April felt a pang of guilt at the hope in the girl's eyes. "Of course, California is a wonderful place to live, too. Your aunt Tracy—"

"Can we just go?" Ranie asked, stomping her boots

against the sidewalk. "I'm going to freeze to death if we stand around any longer."

"Right." April took a breath. "Let's check out a few of the shops." She tugged gently on one of Shay's braids. "There's a great little toy store around the corner."

Shay slipped her hand into Connor's as they started down the sidewalk. "We'll need lots of games and toys so we don't bug you when you're writing the book."

Connor's jaw tightened and April watched him try to pull his hand out of Shay's, but she held tight. "Um... okay."

"You should probably buy us extra. That way we'll be really quiet."

"If that's what it will take," Connor said around a choked laugh.

A laugh. It was like music to April's ears.

"And Ranie wants a new iPad." Shay was skipping now. "If they have those."

"Connor is not buying your sister an iPad," April said quickly.

Ranie glanced back at Shay. "Nice try, though."

They got to the front of the toy shop, and Shay let go of Connor's hand to press her fingers to the glass. "It's a winter wonderland," she said, her tone rapturous.

It was true. The toy store had one of the best window displays in town. It was a mini version of Santa's workshop, with elves positioned around a large table filled with wooden trains and boats and stuffed bears and smiling dolls. Above that scene a sleigh pulled by tiny reindeer was suspended from the ceiling and, from one side, Santa Claus watched the whole scene.

"They have holiday decorations in California," Ranie muttered.

"But it seems more Christmasy when it's cold and snowy," Shay said, and sighed happily. "Like this is a place Santa Claus would live."

Connor cleared his throat. "You know Santa really—"

Ranie stomped on his foot at the same time April elbowed him.

"Hey," he yelled, wincing.

"What were you going to say about Santa?" Shay asked, turning from the window.

"I was going to say that Santa lives at the North Pole." He threw a look to April and then Ranie.

"Sorry," April whispered.

"But," he continued, focusing on Shay. "I'm sure Crimson is one of his favorite stops on Christmas Eve."

She nodded, serious. "So he'll find us even though we're not with Mommy or Aunt Tracy?"

"He'll find you," he assured the girl with a small half smile.

April's heart pounded in her chest. Connor Pierce wasn't as dead on the inside as he pretended to be. The way he looked at Shay convinced her his heart wasn't totally broken. It could be fixed and, because it was her way, she wanted to fix it. To fix him.

The door to the shop opened, several mothers with a gaggle of small children between them spilling out. There was giggling and happy shouts as the group headed down the sidewalk.

"Let's go in," she said, and held the door. Shay ran through and Ranie followed. April glanced back at Connor. He looked as if he'd seen a ghost. His face had gone pale and the lines bracketing his mouth and eyes were, once again, etched deep.

"Are you okay?" She turned to call for Ranie and

Shay, but they'd disappeared into the crowded store. "Let me find the girls and—"

"No." He ran a hand through his dark hair. "I can't go in there. I saw a sporting-goods store on the next block. I'll meet you there." He pulled out his wallet, grabbed a hundred-dollar bill and pressed it into her palm. "Buy them whatever the hell they want to shut them up."

She opened her mouth to argue, but he was already striding away.

"What's wrong with Connor?"

Ranie and Shay had returned to the open doorway, staring at April.

"He needed to...uh..."

"Get away from us," Ranie supplied.

April shook her head and moved into the store. "No, that wasn't it. We'll meet up with him in a bit."

"But I want him to help me pick out a game," Shay said. It was the first time April had heard the young girl whine. "I like him."

Ranie sniffed. "He doesn't like—"

"Then let's pick out some fun stuff," April interrupted. "I'm sure he'll want to see it all."

Ranie rolled her eyes again but led Shay toward the wall of board and card games at the side of the store.

April sighed as she followed them, glancing over her shoulder, hoping to see Connor making his way through the other customers toward her. He wasn't there. Suddenly, all of her hope and holiday spirit seemed insignificant in the face of his overwhelming grief.

Connor ducked into a narrow walkway between two buildings a few storefronts away from the toy shop. He pressed himself against the cold brick and tried to calm the nausea roiling through him. His legs trembled and his heart raced. He could barely catch his breath from the panic choking him.

Why the hell had he agreed to leave the cabin? He'd been a hermit for three years and somehow chosen a popular mountain town two weeks before Christmas as his first outing. A trip to a toy store? What a disaster. There was a reason he lived in seclusion. He wasn't capable of handling anything more. The pounding of his heart was proof of that.

In just one day, April had made him feel more alive than he had since the accident. Like a deluded moth fixated on a bright flame, he'd been stupid enough to believe that meant he had hope. He'd even relaxed around those two girls, almost as broken as him. But an isolated cabin wasn't real life. The prickling under his skin had started the moment he got out of the car and only intensified as Shay took his hand and led him along the crowded street.

The toy store was too much. As soon as he'd heard the children's laughter, which had sounded so much like Emmett's, he'd lost it. Emmett would be almost eight years old now. How would he have changed? Would his sweet laugh have deepened or gotten louder? What would be on his Christmas list? Would his son still believe in Santa Claus?

If Ranie and April hadn't stopped him, Connor would have told Shay there was no Santa. He really was a demented embodiment of Ebenezer Scrooge if he was cracked enough to ruin an innocent girl's belief in Christmas magic.

This was why he was better off alone.

A cold wind rushed between the buildings and he realized he was nearly shivering, more because of the adrenaline draining out of him than the temperature. But he took a deep breath and made his way to the sporting-goods store, feigning interest in a display of backpacks as he worked to regulate his nerves. A well-meaning salesclerk approached him and then quickly backed away at the look Connor shot him. He was holding it together by too thin a thread to make small talk.

A touch on his arm a few minutes later had him spinning around. "I don't need help," he growled, then stopped as April arched a brow.

"That's right," she said softly. "You've got it all under control."

"I shouldn't have come with you today." He glanced over her shoulder to where Ranie and Shay were standing a few feet away, eyeing him warily. Several stuffed shopping bags sat at their feet.

"Maybe not," she agreed, and the fact that she'd already given up on him was an unexpected disappointment.

"Take me back to the cabin," he demanded.

She shook her head. "We're going to the bakery for hot chocolate and muffins and then ice skating."

"I want to go back…" He cleared his throat when several customers glanced their way, and then said in a quieter tone, "I'm the guest."

She took a step closer. "You chose to come with us today, and it's too far to drive you up the mountain and then come back down." Her smile was so sweet it almost made his teeth ache. "Suck it up, Connor," she whispered. "These girls deserve some fun and we're going to give it to them."

He glared but her smile only deepened, daring him to defy her. Somehow that challenge calmed his demons. Everyone else he knew coddled him and, while his grief was real, being handled with kid gloves as if he was liable to crumple at any moment only gave more power to the sorrow slowly eating away at him. For whatever reason, April expected more.

Panic attack be damned, he wanted to give it to her.

He reached out and lifted a lock of her copper hair, rolling the soft strands between his fingers. A blush colored her cheeks and his body went from ice to fire in the span of an instant.

Connor didn't understand what it was about this woman that gentled the pain inside him, but even he wasn't fool enough to walk away. "Okay."

Her lips parted in surprise, and if it wasn't for Ranie and Shay still watching, he would have claimed them as his. He didn't like to be touched but craved contact with April like she was a toddler's well-loved security blanket.

"Let's have some damn fun," he whispered. He grabbed the shopping bags and stalked past the girls back onto the crowded sidewalk.

April pressed her fingers to her forehead as she led her motley crew into the Life is Sweet bakery a few minutes later. Connor was so tense she could almost see it radiating off him like a current. Ranie was back to her normal sulking and even Shay seemed subdued, as if afraid she might set off Connor again and send him running from their little group.

For whatever reason, the young girl felt a connection with the surly, standoffish man. April couldn't explain it any more than she could understand her own attraction to him. Shay had taken great care in picking out toys and games, even adding a few she thought Connor might like to play.

"For when he needs a break," she'd told April shyly.

"That's nice," April had answered, her throat clogging at the girl's inherent generosity.

"When he takes a break, he isn't going to want to hang out with us," Ranie had said. "We're the problem."

"We're not a problem," Shay had argued. "It's just like when Mommy needed rest. After she napped, she was always happy to see us."

"We're everyone's problem," Ranie had said under her breath, but she hadn't corrected Shay.

These three damaged souls were April's responsibility for the next two weeks, and she didn't have a clue how to help them. A trip to town had seemed so simple back at the cabin. But Connor was clearly having difficulty with the crush of holiday shoppers, and his black mood was quickly seeping into the rest of them, like sludge coating everything in its path.

The smell of fresh-baked pastries gave her a bit of hope as the bells over the bakery's door jingled merrily. As usual, Life is Sweet was filled with customers, drawn by the scent and the promise of the town's best cup of coffee. The walls were painted a cheery yellow and cheery spruce garland had been strung from the wooden beams across the ceiling. A tree sat in one corner, decorated with strings of popcorn and cookie cutters tied to bright red ribbon. Who could stay bad-tempered in the face of so much cheer?

Connor Pierce, by the looks of him. He was staring at the other patrons like they were part of the holiday apocalypse and might transform into zombies at any moment.

"I thought you were working at Cloud Cabin this week."

April turned to see Katie Crawford, the bakery's owner, making her way from the display counter toward them. Katie was a Crimson native and, although she knew almost everyone in town, always had room in her life for another friend. One of the best things about coming to Crimson had been having true friends in addition to Sara.

"We came down for a little holiday shopping," April said, stepping forward to hug Katie. "You look amazing."

"I feel like a beached whale." Katie rubbed her round belly and flashed a wry smile. "I'm getting bigger every day. This little guy or girl is kicking all the time."

Katie was almost seven months pregnant with her first baby. "I bet Noah loves that," April answered.

"He sure does," Katie agreed. Her husband, Noah, worked for the Forest Service in town. It was a shared joke among their friends that the man who hadn't taken anything seriously in life for so many years was now an overprotective, earnest father-to-be. "Let me clear off a table for you." She tilted her head toward Connor and the girls. "I didn't realize there was a family staying at the cabin."

Connor's expression tightened further at Katie's suggestion.

April quickly motioned the girls forward. "These are the daughters of a friend of mine. They're staying with me over the holidays." She searched Katie's face, but her friend seemed to accept the simple explanation. April breathed a little sigh of relief. "Ranie and Shay, this is my friend Katie Crawford. She makes everything you see and smell in the bakery."

"Welcome to Crimson," Katie said with a warm smile that even Ranie returned.

As April hoped, it was difficult not to be comforted by the atmosphere of Life is Sweet. Connor still stood stone-faced a couple of feet behind them.

She gave him a pointed look and he moved forward. "This is Connor Pierce, Cloud Cabin's guest."

"Welcome to Crimson," Katie said, shaking his hand. "I hope your Christmas with us is a merry one."

"I'm here to work," he muttered in response.

"That's why Ranie and I have to be quiet," Shay announced. "We got games to keep us busy so we don't bug him."

April saw color rise to Connor's cheeks. At least he had the good sense to be embarrassed.

Katie seemed to take it all in stride. She led them to a table near the window. "Do you want the usual?" she asked April. When April nodded, she turned to the girls. "How about a hot chocolate for each of you?"

Shay smiled. "With whipped cream and marshmallows?"

"Of course." Katie placed her hand on Ranie's shoulder. "What about something to eat?"

"I guess a cookie would be good," Ranie said softly.

"Perfect." Katie clapped her hands together. "I have a batch of chocolate-chip cookies about to come out of the oven. Would you two like to see the kitchen?"

Both girls looked at April.

"Wash your hands when you're back there," she told them.

Katie's gaze shifted to Connor. "For you?"

He looked at his feet. "Nothing."

Katie shot April a questioning look but said only, "Let me know if you change your mind."

The girls took off their bulky coats, then followed Katie through the heavy swinging door that led to the kitchen.

As soon as they were out of sight, April rounded on Connor. "This is *not* sucking it up," she said on a hiss of breath.

"I'm here when I don't want to be," he answered, sinking into one of the café table's metal chairs. "Doesn't that count?"

April sat next to him. "No."

He glanced up at her.

"I mean it, Connor." She peeled off her gloves and set them on the tabletop.

He blew out a breath. "I'm sorry. I really am. I thought I could have a normal afternoon, but there's nothing normal about me, April. It's not an accident that I keep to myself. You can see I'm not fit to be around people." A muscle ticked in his jaw, and he looked so miserable that she felt a stab of sympathy for him.

"When was the last time you did something social?"

He gave a harsh laugh. "Does a funeral count?"

"Oh, Connor."

"Don't feel sorry for me," he whispered. "Those girls need and want your sympathy. I'm fine the way I am."

But he was the opposite of fine, and April hated it.

Hated that he had no one in his life to pull him away from his grief, even if he went kicking and screaming.

What she'd been through was nothing compared to his experience, but she wondered if she would have fallen into a deeper sorrow for what she'd lost if she hadn't had Sara to look after her. What about Ranie and Shay? Was having each other enough to see them through the pain of their mother's death?

All of her frustrations bubbled to the surface before she could rein them in. "I guess I don't need to feel sorry for you when you do such a bang-up job of it yourself."

His gaze crashed into hers. "I don't feel sorry for myself."

She knew she should stop talking but couldn't seem to keep her mouth shut. "I can't imagine what you've been through, but you hold on to your isolation like it's a precious gift. Is that what your wife would have wanted for you?"

He went absolutely still, and she realized she'd crossed some invisible line. "You know nothing about her," he whispered, his voice raw.

"You're right," she continued, despite the warning bells going off in her head. "But if she loved you half as much as you loved her, she would have wanted you to be happy. To cherish her memory and your son's by living, Connor. Not by—"

"Stop." He slammed his palm onto the table. "I can't be happy. I won't let myself."

People from the tables around them stared, but April ignored everything except the man sitting across from her. Pain was etched into every inch of his face. "Why?" she whispered.

"Because," he answered, drawing in a ragged breath, "it would mean I've let go of Margo and Emmett. I won't lose them any more than I already have."

The honesty in that statement sliced through her. This was Connor, tied to tragedy and holding on to the past even though it kept him from living now. By the time she'd gathered her composure to argue, he'd stood.

"I don't want to ruin the girls' fun this afternoon. They should have a chance to be happy again, and you can help them. But not me, April. There's no help for me."

"That's not true."

He reached down and pressed a finger to her lips. The gentle touch sent a shock wave of longing through her. His skin was warm, so at odds with the ice in his voice. "Enjoy your time here. Take them skating. I'll meet you back at the car when you're finished."

And he walked away.

Tears clogged April's throat and she focused on her breathing as a server brought two hot chocolates and her tea to the table. What if she couldn't help him? What if he was meant to be locked in that self-imposed prison for the rest of his life? The thought rocked her to her core. She didn't want the connection she felt to Connor, but she didn't want to let it go.

A few minutes later Katie and the girls returned to the table. Ranie and Shay each held a plate with two cookies.

"Look at all that whipped cream," Shay cried as she slipped into a seat and then stuck out her tongue to lick off one of the chocolate shavings. "Marshmallows, too. This is the best."

Ranie's gaze darted around the bakery as she sat. "Where is he?"

"He had some things to do in town."

"Things like avoiding us," Ranie mumbled.

April threw a helpless smile at Katie. "Merry Christmas," she whispered.

"That's the famous author, right?"

April nodded.

"He's different than I imagined, based on his books," Katie said gently. Thanks to its proximity to Aspen, Crimson saw plenty of famous visitors each year. Most people in town took it in stride.

"I think he's different than he used to be," April answered.

Shay dipped a spoon into the hot chocolate and scooped up a mini marshmallow. "He's grumpy because he has so much work to do."

April placed a hand on the girl's thin shoulder. "Sweetie, it's more than the work. Connor had a wife and son who died in a car accident a few years ago. He misses them."

Shay nodded. "I miss Mommy. It's sad when people die."

April saw Katie's eyes widen. Maybe it had been a mistake to come to town, after all. Sara might be on vacation, but there were plenty of other friends she'd need to avoid if she didn't want to talk about the situation with Ranie and Shay. Her reputation in town was that of a mother hen, the one who took care of everyone around her. While that might be true for her friends, she couldn't imagine allowing the girls to stay with her permanently.

April had arranged her life so that *permanent* wasn't

part of it. She had no real commitments to anyone or anything, and if that was a bit lonely, it was also safer. She couldn't be hurt if she wasn't truly involved.

"It is sad," she told Shay. "So we'll have to be extra patient with Connor."

"Even though," Ranie piped in, "he's a big jerk."

April didn't bother to correct her. "Even though," she agreed, and earned the ghost of a smile from Ranie. That was something.

She glanced up at Katie, who was eyeing the three of them curiously. "You should call me later," her friend said, clearly interested in the story April wasn't sharing.

"Service is spotty at the cabin." April sipped her tea.

Katie frowned. "There's a landline, right?"

"Thank you for cookies and drinks," April answered, ignoring the question. She pulled her wallet from her purse, but Katie shook her head.

"A Christmas present for your guests."

Both girls thanked Katie, who was still studying them as if trying to puzzle out the deeper meaning. April felt herself tense, but at that moment one of the women behind the counter called to Katie.

"You go on," April told her. "The bakery is slammed, and they need you."

Katie hesitated.

April finally relented. "I'll call you soon."

With a satisfied nod, Katie hugged both girls and then April. "You've supported every single friend you've made in town these past few years," she said, her dark brown eyes sincere. "Maybe it's time you let us return the favor."

"Thank you," April whispered, hating that her voice shook a little.

When Katie walked away, she plastered the smile back on her face. "Who's up for ice skating?"

Chapter Five

Connor had walked the streets surrounding downtown Crimson since leaving the bakery and was now
cold to the bone. He hadn't worn gloves or a hat, and
both his fingers and head felt practically frozen. He'd
lived his whole life in northern California, so while
he was used to damp cold, the bone-chilling air of the
Colorado mountains was an entirely new sensation.

One plus to turning into a human Popsicle was that
it had helped him get his burning emotions back under
control. He'd had to get away from the crowds and
April's too-knowing gaze. Not because she was out of
line in speaking about Margo and Emmett but because
the truth in her words shamed him.

Margo would have wanted him to go on with his
life and find happiness again. Her parents had visited
him several times after the funeral to try to convince

him of just that. April and those girls made him smile, lifted his heart out of the blackness that had surrounded it for so long. But it felt like a betrayal to his wife and son's memory to feel anything but emptiness.

He dug his knuckles into his chest, trying to keep everything buried. Alone in his small apartment north of San Francisco, it had been easy to pretend that sorrow and guilt were all there was to him. It was the only way to make sure he would never again feel the pain of so much loss.

He made his way from the picturesque residential neighborhood with cozy houses decorated with lights and garlands back toward the equally charming business district and came to stand at the edge of the outdoor ice rink. The rink was large, occupying most of a public park that stretched the length of a city block. Many groups of skaters twirled around the wide oval shape. He spotted April and Shay on the far side of the rink, holding hands and moving slowly. April looked steady on her skates, but Shay was hanging off her arm as if April was the only thing balancing the girl.

He scanned the other skaters but couldn't find Ranie. Finally he noticed her bright blue parka at the edge of the rink. He could see her gripping the edge of the wall, but she wasn't moving and her face was buried in her arms. Without thinking, he started toward her.

"You'd better get going," he said when he was in front of her across the wall. "This is a skating rink, not a parking lot." She didn't move and he immediately regretted the stupid joke. His brilliant social skills were making a mess of things once again.

When she raised her head to glare at him, her cheeks

were stained with tears. His heart lurched. Still not as dead on the inside as he wanted to be.

"Hey," he said, placing his hand awkwardly on her arm. She jerked away, then started to lose her balance and reached for him. He grabbed both her arms and held on tight. "I'm sorry. Bad joke."

"I don't care about anything you say," she snapped. "I can't skate."

"Well, you're holding on to the wall like a champ, so you must have gotten this far somehow."

She shook her head. "I'm stuck here. I can't move."

"Sure you can." He loosened his grip on her. "I'm going to let go and—"

"No!" Her voice was pure panic.

"It's okay," he said. "I've got you." He looked for April's copper hair amid the skaters gliding toward them but couldn't see her. At the speed she and Shay were moving, it would take another several minutes for them to make it to this end of the rink.

"I'll fall if you let go."

"You were doing fine before I got here."

"I wasn't."

"Everyone falls when learning to skate, Ranie. A few bruises and you'll be fine."

"I'm afraid. Please help me, Connor." She sounded miserable, whether from her fear or having to ask him for help, he couldn't tell.

He should have kept walking. He didn't want to be involved, but he couldn't make himself desert this girl now. Not when he could actually help her. The fact that she would rely on him, even if only because she was desperate, poked at something deep inside him. It was

nothing, an inconsequential turn around a skating rink.
But it was something he could do.

"I'm going to let you go and—"

"Fine. Who needs you anyway?" She bit down on
her lip.

"For a second while I hop over the wall."

"Oh." She nodded and took a breath.

He hitched her up so she could hang on to the wall
while he boosted himself up and over. His boots slid
as they hit the ice, and he very nearly landed flat on
his back. After righting himself, Connor took hold of
Ranie's arm. "Let go now."

"I can't," she whispered. "I'll fall."

He bent and wrapped his arm around her waist, pulling her closer to him. He hadn't been this near another
person, let alone a child, since the accident.

"I've got you, Ranie. Trust me."

Those were the wrong words, because Connor
wasn't someone this girl should trust. But she lifted
her hands from the wall, grabbing tightly to his coat
sleeve. Her whole body was stiff as he walked across
the ice, dragging her along with him as he went. The
rink seemed even more crowded now, and he focused
on moving through the center to make a small circle
that would put them back at the break in the wall that
served as the skaters' entrance and exit. He glanced at
the frightened girl still holding on to him and saw that
her eyes were squeezed shut.

"Not much of a skater?" he asked, keeping his tone
conversational.

She gave a sharp shake of her head.

"Why did you agree to this little outing anyway?"

"Shay was excited. She's never ice-skated. And

April really wanted to make her happy after you were such a jerk."

He smiled at her blunt words. "This wasn't your first time?"

"No."

"Bad experience?" He steered her toward the edge of the rink. "Open your eyes. We're almost to the exit."

She did and let out a shuddery breath. He stepped onto the rubber mat in front of the exit and helped Ranie off the ice. The girl took two steps forward and sank onto one of the metal benches surrounding the rink. Connor glanced over his shoulder and caught April's gaze. She held Shay's hand, the young girl smiling from ear to ear as they sailed over the ice. He could read the question in her eyes but motioned for her to take another turn around the rink. He expected her to ignore him, but instead she and Shay glided past the break in the wall.

Connor looked down at Ranie, who had her elbows on her knees and her face in her hands. Panic licked down his spine. Why the hell hadn't he let April take over? Clearly, the girl was upset about something and he was wholly ill equipped to deal with whatever it was.

With a sigh, he sat down next to her. "Tell me about you and skating."

She shook her head.

"That's okay. I'm happy to think you're a wimpy girl."

She sucked in a breath and dropped her hands. "You really are a jerk," she said, glaring at him.

He nodded. "Are you going to tell me?"

"It's stupid."

"I guess you want me to think you're wimpy *and* stupid?"

She mumbled something under her breath that he pretended not to hear. "My mom took me skating when I was little. Shay was a tiny baby and Mom got a baby-sitter for her so we could have a fun afternoon together. It was an indoor rink because we were in California, but she fell and sprained her wrist."

"And that scared you?"

The girl shrugged. "Maybe. I don't remember. She went to the doctor for a splint and asked them about a lump she had under her arm. That's when we found out she had cancer."

Again Connor wished he hadn't waved April away. And why had she listened to him? He was the last thing this girl needed right now. He scrubbed a hand through his hair and whispered, "That sucks." It was all he could think of at the moment.

Ranie gave a small laugh. "You're bad at giving comfort."

"No doubt," he agreed.

"But thank you for rescuing me."

"What happened out there?"

"I don't know." Her thin shoulders slumped like they carried the weight of the world. "I didn't think it was a big deal, but I started skating and suddenly I was afraid. Like something bad might happen if I fell. I'm all Shay has left and…" She broke off, wiped a mit-tened hand across her cheeks, then said, "You're right. I'm stupid and wimpy."

Connor cringed. "I didn't say that exactly."

She rolled her eyes. "You sort of did."

"I was trying to get you to talk to me."

"I know." She sighed. "I bet you regret it now."

He stood and turned to her. "Hold that thought." He jogged over to the ticket booth, grabbed his wallet from his back pocket and then pushed a few bills toward the teenager working behind the counter. He told her his shoe size and, skates in hand, returned to the bench next to Ranie.

"What are you doing?"

"I'm putting on ice skates."

"You're going to leave me and go skating after what I just told you?"

He cut her a look. "No, we're both going back out there."

"No way." Ranie crossed her arms over her chest, the puffy down jacket making her look more substantial than she was.

Both Ranie and Shay were delicate and fine-boned, much like April, although they weren't related. Emmett had been solidly built, "husky" as the clothes Margo bought for him were called. Connor had mistakenly thought that the boy's sturdy body would keep him safe, but there wasn't much anyone could do when jackknifed on the highway on a rainy night.

The familiar wave of grief pounded him, making it difficult to suck air into his lungs, and he closed his eyes and prepared for it to take him under.

"Hey."

He felt a gentle nudge on his arm. Blinking several times, he opened his eyes to find Ranie staring up at him. His sorrow started the slow slide back into the dark crevice that was its home.

"I'll go with you," she said, "Just don't look like you're going to freak out on me."

"I'm not going to freak out," he muttered.

"Right. Because this moment is about *me*. This is my freak-out. You got yours earlier."

He couldn't help but smile at her attitude. "Are you distracting me?"

"I think we're distracting each other," she told him, and looped her hand around his elbow. "You better not let me fall."

He led her toward the ice. "The whole purpose is to get okay with falling."

April and Shay met them at the edge of the rink. They moved so that they weren't blocking the steady stream of skaters getting on and off the rink. Ranie didn't let go of his arm.

"What's going on?" April asked, eyeing the two of them like she wasn't sure what to make of them together. Connor understood the sentiment.

"Connor is teaching me to ice-skate."

"You told April you didn't need help," Shay said. "She can teach you. She's good." She tugged at Ranie's free arm. "Better than him."

"No doubt," Connor agreed, earning a frown from both April and Ranie. How was it that those two weren't related when they could give such well-matched death glares? He sighed, maneuvered Ranie so she could hold on to the wall and crouched down in front of Shay. "You look like a pro out there, Shay," he said. "I bet this isn't your first time on skates."

"Is so," she said, chewing on her bottom lip and looking over his shoulder. Her nose and cheeks were bright pink and her blond hair had escaped its braid to curl around the edges of the knit cap she wore. After a moment she met his gaze. "April taught me. She's nice."

Connor understood that part of what she was thinking went unsaid. "I'm sorry I wasn't nice earlier." Despite the cold, he felt a bead of sweat roll between his shoulder blades. Her innocence reminded him so much of his son. But both April and Ranie were right. He'd had a time for his own freak-out, and there would be plenty more once he was alone again.

As difficult as it was, for two weeks he could help these girls maneuver through this new life without their mother. It's what Margo would have expected from him and what he'd wish for his own son if the situation was reversed. The familiar rhythm of wanting to change the past pounded in his chest, but he forced it away. "Sometimes when I'm sad it makes me grumpy."

"You're sad because your family died."

He swallowed. "Yes."

"I bet you were nice to them."

"I tried to be," he whispered. "I loved them very much, just like your mommy loved you." He slipped off his glove and reached out to touch the tip of her nose. "I'm going to try to be nicer to everyone because my wife and son would have wanted that."

"Mommy made videos and wrote letters for Ranie and me to look at on our birthdays every year. She said she'll tell us things we need to know like how to make friends and be smart and stuff." She smiled. "You can teach Ranie to skate, but I still bet you're not as good as April."

"I'm not that great," April said as Connor straightened.

He met her dark gaze. "You looked pretty darn good to me."

"Oh," she whispered, color rising to her cheeks.

Ranie gave a patented teenage groan. "Let's go before I freeze even more."

Connor winked at April, surprised he could still make the gesture, and led Ranie back onto the ice.

"You're giving me whiplash," April said as she and Connor stood behind the skating rink's wall and watched Shay and Ranie circle the rink.

Connor shot her a look out of the corner of his eye. "I'm not even moving."

"It's your attitude. You need to pick whether you're going to be a jerk or a decent human being. This back-and-forth is making me crazy."

Crazy might be an understatement for how she felt with Connor. Earlier today she'd written him off after he'd stalked away at the bakery. She'd figured her attempt at drawing him out of his isolation had failed and she'd maneuver through the Christmas holiday as best she could. Until he'd shown up at the ice rink, patiently taught Ranie how to skate, and then spun and raced with Shay while the young girl giggled. Ranie had actually laughed and, once she felt comfortable, the girl was a natural on skates. There was a connection between these girls and Connor that April didn't understand but could still appreciate.

He'd been so gentle with the girl the first time she'd fallen. After a few moments Ranie had gotten up with a huge smile on her face, dusted the ice off her legs and kept going. It was the tenderness that affected April the most. She could deal with moody Connor and even handle her attraction to him. But the gentleness was so at odds with who he pretended to be that it slid into her soul and made her want more than either one of them was willing to give.

"I'm out of practice with the human part," he said quietly.

"Yet suddenly you're willing to work on it?"

He turned to her more fully. "Isn't that what you wanted?"

She sucked in a deep breath of the cold mountain air, hoping the pain in her lungs would help clear her mind and make sense of the emotions tumbling through her.

"Yes," she said after a moment.

"But..."

But she was afraid. Afraid to trust her feelings after so long, especially when they could only lead to disappointment. Afraid to admit how much she cared for those girls after only a short time with them. Giving them back was going to be the hardest thing she'd ever done, but she still didn't have a choice.

If her cancer had taught her one thing it was that life was uncertain, and April's life most of all. She'd tried making plans, had had her future mapped out and it had all turned to hell, leaving her alone and heartbroken. She couldn't risk that again. In some ways it was easier with Connor as the bad guy. She could concentrate on his issues instead of her own failings. But a Connor willing to try was another thing entirely.

"I'm glad," she answered finally.

"You're a bad liar," he said with a small laugh, and tucked a loose strand of hair behind her ear. He wasn't wearing gloves and she loved the warmth of his finger where it touched her cold skin.

She'd stuffed her hat in her pocket after coming off the ice and now brushed her hair over one shoulder, then waved to the girls as they skated by. "I'm sure I have terrible hat hair."

"You look beautiful." His hand slid around the back of her neck and pulled her closer. Nerves zipped around her stomach and she gazed into his dark eyes. "I don't want to fight with you." His lips brushed against hers, soft for a man with so many hard angles.

"I work for you, Connor."

He nipped at the edge of her mouth. "You work for Crimson Ranch."

"You're the guest," she whispered, but when he would have pulled back she fused her mouth to his. It was reckless, but the past few years of being alone had suddenly become too much. She needed to kiss Connor Pierce like she needed her next breath.

It was everything she'd imagined and nothing she expected. His lips were gentle, searching. He made her feel that they had all day to savor each other, instead of a few stolen moments while the girls were busy on the ice. He slanted his mouth over hers, but all too soon they broke apart.

"I like being the guest," he whispered as his hands dropped away.

Her head felt fuzzy and she touched her fingertips to her lips, surprised they seemed to be the same as they were minutes earlier. Foolish as it was, that kiss had released something inside her that she hadn't realized she'd shut away. It was more than awareness or attraction. She wanted Connor even though, in Crimson, she'd built her life around supporting others, never taking anything for herself.

He waved to the girls and she fought to regain her composure as they came off the ice.

"I'm getting cold," Shay said, her teeth chattering. The sun had just started to dip behind the mountain and the temperature was already dropping. April was used to the double-digit fluctuations in temperature from day to night in the mountains, but it was often a surprise to people new to Colorado. "Can we go home now?"

Home.

The truth came rushing back to April as guilt hit her like a punch to the gut. These girls had no home and neither did she. Yes, she had a cozy apartment in town but it wasn't the same as a home. Not for her. It was a place to keep her belongings and a base of operations. Nothing more. She hadn't had a real home since she'd packed her bags and walked out of the sprawling Mediterranean house she'd shared with her husband.

The fact that Shay could lose her mother and be taken from the only home she'd ever known and, in the space of a day, think of a temporary cabin as home humbled April. She was used to friends coming to her for advice but realized she had so much to learn about hope and resilience from these girls.

"Yes," she said, swallowing around the lump in her throat. "Let's go home."

They walked to the car in the waning afternoon light, Shay chattering the whole way as she held on to Connor's hand. A few kind words and all was forgiven. April wished it was so easy as an adult.

Ranie, who was leading the way down the sidewalk, suddenly stopped. "Be quiet," she said on a hiss of breath. "Listen."

All four of them stood in silence next to the Jeep.

"I don't hear anything," April whispered, but then she did. A tiny sound. Definitely a meow.

Oh, no.

Ranie held out her hand, eyes trained on the snow-covered garbage can near the corner. Dark was coming now and shadows filled the space under and around the metal can. "Give me your phone. Please."

April dug in her purse and then handed it over.

The girl flipped on the flashlight app and shone the light toward the trash can. Two yellow eyes stared out at them.

Connor moved closer and crouched down.

"Be careful," April whispered.

Connor threw her a look. "It's a kitten."

"It *sounds* like a kitten," April argued. "Who knows if—"

Shay clapped her hands. "It's a kitten," she shouted as Connor pulled the small animal out from under the trash can.

"Shh." Ranie handed the phone back to April before taking the bundle of fluff from Connor. "You'll scare him."

"He's tiny," Shay whispered, her eyes double their normal size.

"He's freezing." Ranie tucked the small animal into her parka.

"Me, too," her sister said.

April hit the remote-start button on her key fob. "Everyone in the car. We'll think better when we're warm."

The girls climbed into the backseat while she and Connor got in the front. She flipped on the overhead light and turned toward the girls. "There's an animal shelter just outside of town. If I call now—"

Ranie shook her head and kept her gaze on the kitten. All April could see was a tuft of black hair peeking out of her coat.

"We have to keep him," Shay whispered, reaching out a finger to stroke the kitten's fur.

"He needs to see a vet."

"We'll take him on the way home."

April threw Connor a "help me" look.

"What will you name him?" he asked.

"Not funny." April swatted his arm. "Girls, you can't keep him."

"Sure we can," Ranie said, finally glancing up. "If you say yes. He's purring."

"I can hear him," Shay said. "Can I hold him?"

Ranie shook her head. "Not until we get back to the cabin. He's warm in my coat."

"He can be warm in my coat."

"We're not taking him to the cabin," April told them, struggling to keep her voice even. "We're taking him to the animal shelter." She pulled out her phone. "I know the woman who runs it. She does a great job matching animals with homes."

"He has a home," Shay announced. "With us." April started to argue just as the girl added, "Mommy sent him."

"Well played," Connor whispered under his breath.

April narrowed her eyes at him, then adjusted in her seat so she could talk directly to the girls. The car had warmed enough that she could no longer see her breath, and both Ranie and Shay had pink-tinged cheeks and shiny eyes.

"What do you mean?"

"I told Mommy I wanted a puppy for Christmas, but she said they were too much work but maybe we could get a kitten."

April bit the inside of her cheek to keep from cursing. "When did she tell you that?"

"Halloween." Shay smiled. "I dressed up like a doggy." She petted the kitten's head again. "But I love cats, too."

At the end of October Jill would have known only a miracle could ensure another Christmas with her girls. The fact that she'd made the promise at that point in her illness was so like her. And now April was here to deal with the aftermath and this sweet girl's expectations.

She glanced at Connor. "You can't think it's a good idea that we bring a kitten to the cabin."

"It's not coming to my cabin." He shrugged. "Besides, I like cats."

"If Connor Grumpy Pants likes cats, we have to keep him," Ranie said with a giggle.

Connor pointed at her. "Respect your elders."

She only laughed more.

April shook her head. How had she become the outsider in this group? She straightened in her seat and wrapped her fingers around the steering wheel. She'd gone from being responsible for herself to worrying about these girls, this man and now a kitten.

"We still have to get to a vet," she muttered. "I don't know a lot about cats, but that kitten is just a baby. He should be with his mama."

"Ranie's his mama now," Shay said, wonder in her voice. "I'm his auntie. What if he's a girl?"

"The vet will be able to tell us," Connor offered. "Maybe you should wait to name him until we find out."

"This doesn't mean I'm keeping him forever," April said as she threw the car into gear and eased onto the road. The traffic in the downtown had lightened as darkness unfolded. She flicked a glance at the clock on the dash. "One of the local vets is a yoga client of mine. We'll head to her office."

"Sucker," Connor whispered.

April rolled her eyes. "You know the constant commentary doesn't help."

"It makes me happy, and it's good when the guest is happy."

An hour later and a hundred dollars lighter, April pointed her car toward Crimson Mountain. Darkness had fallen completely and only the muted silhouette of the peak was visible under the soft moonlight. The wide-open spaces they drove past on either side of the highway were dotted with the soft glow of the various properties situated outside of town. Sometimes when she'd driven back to town from Crimson Ranch, she'd thought about the houses filled with happy families gathered around their kitchen tables and imagined what it would be like to have a family of her own.

Now she had a full car and more people depending on her than she would have ever guessed, not to mention a new pet. She almost giggled from the absurdity of the way her life had changed so quickly. Oblivious to her musings, the girls sat in the backseat, both of their heads bent over the kitten, which now slept in a tiny ball curled inside Shay's jacket.

It had taken quite a bit of coaxing for Ranie to share

him. The girl had kept the kitten, whom they'd named Jingle after he was confirmed a boy, close during the visit to the vet and a trip to the local pet store for supplies.

The vet had guessed him to be about seven weeks old, too young to be away from his mama and littermates. But he was on his own, so they'd received instructions on how to care for a baby kitten, and even purchased a bottle from the pet shop so the girls could feed him with it.

April felt a bit of panic at the thought of all it would take to keep the small ball of fluff alive and healthy in the next few weeks. She liked animals and dog-sat for a few of her friends, but she'd never been solely responsible for an animal. Growing up, her mother had been fastidious about the house and had never entertained the idea of a pet. Even a goldfish had been deemed too much mess. Her ex-husband had felt the same way, and April had never questioned either rule or the fact that she had no input making it.

Now she knew why. The kitten terrified her.

"He's going to be fine," Connor said softly, as if he could read her thoughts. "If he survived living under that trash can, your cabin is going to seem like the Taj Mahal."

She adjusted the radio so that the sound was playing from the speakers in the back of the SUV and turned up the volume. "I can't keep him," she whispered, sliding a glance at Connor, "and I doubt the girls' aunt will let them bring him to her house."

"Then think of it as being a foster mom for a couple of weeks. He's with you until he's old enough to be adopted by a family who wants him."

"Do you have any pets at home?"

His mouth thinned. "Not anymore."

April sucked in a breath. "You don't mean—"

"My wife, Margo, had a dog. He'd been hers before we were married and was almost twelve. She loved that mutt like a second child. After the accident, I couldn't—" He broke off, cleared his throat. "Her parents took him. It gave them some comfort to take care of something she'd loved so much."

"But not you?"

He cleared his throat. "I didn't deserve any comfort."

The words broke another piece of her heart for this man. She reached for his hand just as headlights from the other side of the two-lane highway cut through the night. At the same time, the Jeep's headlights caught on a huge shape in the middle of the highway. A few stray elk crossing. April slammed on the brakes and dimly registered Shay's high-pitched scream as the back end of the SUV fishtailed across a patch of ice.

Luckily, most of the road was dry and the car lurched to a stop as one of the massive animals turned to look at her. Illuminated in the beam of headlights, the elk's dark eyes shone. It paused for only a moment, then trotted across the double yellow line and off the shoulder to follow the others. The truck on the other side of the road had skidded across the median, and then jackknifed directly in her path. The driver rolled down his window and waved before taking off again.

Forcing her fingers to relax their death grip on the steering wheel, she pulled off the highway onto the gravel shoulder. She flipped on the car's interior light and turned to the backseat. "We're fine," she said, meeting both Ranie and Shay's frightened gazes. "Clearly, I still have a ways to go at mastering the art of winter driving in Colorado. Is the kitten safe?"

Shay nodded, opening her arms to show the small animal sleeping peacefully. April smiled despite the adrenaline pounding through her. Her smile disappeared when she flicked a glance at Connor. He sat completely still, staring unfocused out the windshield into the darkness. His fingers were pressed to either side of his temple like his head was pounding.

"It's okay," she whispered, placing her hand on his arm.

He flinched away from her touch. "Get me to the cabin," he said through clenched teeth.

She realized in an instant that whatever he was seeing out the front of the SUV had nothing to do with tonight and everything that involved the accident that had claimed his family. Once again, she wanted to wrap him in her arms and offer whatever comfort she could. Whatever he would take.

"Connor, this wasn't the same—"

"Now," he demanded. "Drive me back now."

The range of emotions in his voice overwhelmed her. Desperation. Panic. Anger. Worse was the fear pouring off him in waves, as if it were a physical force she could reach out and touch. It felt like he was holding on to his composure—and maybe his sanity—by the thinnest thread.

Pulling back onto the darkened highway, she pasted a smile on her face. "Well, this day has turned out to be quite an adventure," she said brightly to the girls.

Shay smiled back at her in the rearview mirror, but Ranie was watching Connor.

"That's one resilient little cat," April continued, hitting the button to turn off the interior light. She had a feeling Connor needed the darkness outside to mask whatever demons were pummeling him from the inside.

He'd made progress today. All of them had. Despite her doubts, she'd wanted to believe there had been some real healing. Now she worried that for the man sitting next to her, any effort she made might never be enough.

Chapter Six

"How's the kitten?"

At the sound of Connor's voice, April whirled around in the cabin's quiet kitchen. The plate she was unloading from the dishwasher crashed to the floor and splintered into a dozen pieces, much like her nerves.

She hadn't seen Connor since they'd returned from town to Cloud Cabin two days ago. He'd darted from the Jeep even before she'd come to a complete stop and disappeared without another word. The girls and the cat had needed her attention, so she'd settled them in the caretaker's cabin before returning to the main cabin to look for him. But there had been no answer when she'd called his name. Obviously, he was there. Where else would he have gone? But as much as she wanted to force him to talk to her, it wasn't her place.

What did she have to offer him anyway?

She'd made a simple dinner of soup and salad and

left it on a tray outside the bedroom door, then returned to her cabin to make dinner for the girls. She'd come back after they'd gone to bed to find the dishwasher loaded and running but no other outward signs of him.

She'd been tempted to call Sara on her vacation and walk away from this job. They'd been here less than a week. Surely Sara could find someone to take April's place. She could move the girls to her small apartment in town or get in the car and drive to the coast. They could rent a house on the beach for the holiday, something that felt like a vacation. Something that wouldn't feel like real life or a glimpse at a future she was too scared to grasp.

But she hadn't made the call.

Instead, she'd left a written schedule of when she would come to the cabin to make meals and check in each day. She figured if he needed her beyond that— and her foolish heart had hoped he might—he could walk across the driveway to her cabin.

Of course he hadn't. Other than the clean dishes in the dishwasher and a light under his bedroom door, there was no indication anyone was in the house. Last night she'd awakened at three o'clock and gone to her window to check the main cabin. The soft yellow glow had illuminated the pure blackness of the forest at night. It seemed appropriate that the cabin remain dark other than that one shining beacon, so she'd taken to working with only the small pendant above the sink to light her way when she came over before sunrise.

Now he stood in the doorway of the kitchen and flipped on the recessed lights. He wore a loose pair of fleece pants and a white T-shirt that was—damn him—fitted across his broad chest and shoulders in a way that made her mouth go dry. His hair was rumpled like he'd been regularly running a hand through it, and the dark stubble that covered his jaw was quickly turning into a beard.

He looked wild and more than a little dangerous, a strange glint in his green eyes as his gaze raked over her. She'd tossed her down parka over the back of one of the kitchen chairs and wanted to hop over the pieces of scattered plate to wrap it around her.

He arched a brow. "Do you always wear pajamas on the job?" His voice was back to a gravelly rumble. It made parts of her body come to attention, parts that she wished would ignore Connor Pierce.

"Are you done hiding?" she shot back. Tearing her gaze from him, she stepped to the pantry and pulled out the broom and dustpan. When she turned around, he was gone, and she hated the instant disappointment that fluttered through her.

But then he returned, walking toward her with so much purpose she actually took a step back. "Let me clean up," he said, pointing to her bare feet. "You're not wearing shoes."

All business. Right. She handed him the broom and dustpan, careful to make sure their fingers didn't brush. "I took off my boots at the door," she said, proud that her tone was even and emotionless. "Jingle is fine, and I'm in my pajamas because I wasn't expecting to see you. You've been like a ghost with an appetite."

His head was bent as he swept, but she saw one corner of his mouth twitch. "Nice unicorns," he said softly.

She ran a hand over the well-worn cotton of her favorite pajamas. They had pictures of unicorns jumping over rainbows covering them, a gift from Sara after April's surgery.

"Did you really leave your inner sanctum to poke fun at my pajamas?"

"No, but it's a bonus." He swept the broken dish pieces into the dustpan, and she pulled out the drawer that held the trash can so he could dump everything in it. He leaned the broom against the counter. "I need to get the vacuum and go over the floor. There may be pieces I missed."

"I can—" April lost her train of thought, yelping as Connor took a step toward her and lifted her into his arms. She was pressed against him from chest to toe, and the scent of mint and spice swirled around her.

After moving her to the far side of the kitchen, away from any remaining shards, he released her. She forced her knees not to buckle. "Don't walk in here without shoes until it's been vacuumed."

"You can't pick me up like that." She patted her fingers to her chest, hoping that would calm her pounding heart. Her reaction to this man was intolerable when he obviously didn't have the same response to her. "I'm not a child."

"You're light as one," he said, scrubbing a hand over his jaw.

The scratching sound was like some sort of unwelcome mating call and April fidgeted as heat pooled low in her belly. First thing to add to her list of New Year's resolutions was finally allowing Sara to set her up on a date with one of Josh's bull-riding friends. Clearly, self-enforced celibacy had negative ramifications.

"What are you thinking?" Connor asked, his voice tinged with amusement.

No way was she sharing her thoughts with him at this moment. Instead, she said, "I'll get the vacuum."

He grabbed her wrist as she moved past. "I wanted to thank you."

She stilled, staring at where his big hand gripped her wrist, olive toned against her pale skin. How could someone who admittedly spent most of his time indoors have such beautifully colored skin?

"April," he whispered, "look at me."

Glancing up through her lashes, she sucked in a breath when her gaze met his. For once, his eyes weren't guarded, and the look he gave her was so tender and intense it made her dizzy with longing.

Stupid longing.

"Thank you for taking care of me these past couple of days."

She sniffed. "It's my job."

He acknowledged her words with a small nod, or maybe it was the bitterness creeping into her tone that he recognized. "How are Ranie and Shay?"

"Do you really care?"

"Yes." He sighed. "Even though I don't want to care. The other night...on the highway...it affected me. Hearing that scream when the car slid on the road and the headlights moving closer." He paused and a shudder ran through him. "I'm sorry I disappeared, but I wasn't fit company for anyone after that."

"It's fine." She tried to hold on to her anger even as it slipped through her body like grains of sand through her fingers. She needed that anger. It was safer with this man. Safer for her heart. "You don't owe me an explanation."

"I want to give you one anyway." His hold on her

gentled and he rubbed his thumb over the sensitive flesh on the inside of her wrist. "I've missed you, April. I've spent the past three years alone, and suddenly I'm lonely without you. I stopped caring. I didn't think I had it in me to care, and I'm still so turned around. Every little thing sets me off and I can't stop it. But I also can't stop wanting to be near you. It doesn't make sense."

She closed her eyes against the onslaught of emotions that poured through her at his words and the gentle pressure to her skin.

"Do you know," he asked, shifting so close now that she could feel his breath against her hair, "that I listen for the door to close after you leave and rush down to the kitchen because your scent lingers after you're gone?"

She huffed out a laugh that sounded breathless to her own ears. "Are you saying I smell?"

"Like lavender and vanilla. I've made an idiot of myself the past two days following traces of you around the house."

"Why are you telling me this?"

"Because I want you to know what you do to me, even if I should stay away. It's better for both of us if I turn around and walk back to my bedroom until you're gone."

She waited a moment, but he didn't move. "You're not walking."

"Hell if I can make myself go."

"Don't go," she whispered. Slowly, as if she were gentling a stray animal, she lifted her hand. Her finger brushed the prickly strands of his dark beard, and his lips parted.

"I forgot to shave," he muttered.

"Too busy?"

He took a breath, released it and then nodded. "Writing."

"Connor," April whispered. "That's wonderful."

He shrugged and looked away. "Who knows how long it will last. But the words are coming. So damn many, drowning me with their force. It's like…"

She pressed her palm to his cheek, gratified when he leaned into it. "Like what?"

"Like it used to be." He said the words softly, as if they were an apology. April could feel the tension in his body and wished, just for a moment, she could transfer his pain to herself. Give him a few seconds of remembering what it was like to live without the weight of guilt and sorrow bearing down on him.

"Look at me," she said, moving closer to him, pressing into his warmth. His arms came around her waist, his hands splayed open against her back. She could feel their heat and strength through the thin cotton of her pajama shirt. So much talent flowed out of those hands. The worlds he created within his imagination and put on paper for readers to discover. "You have a gift, Connor Pierce."

"It's not—"

"Don't say it. Whatever you're thinking." She brushed her lips over his. "Those words are in you. The stories you write are part of you."

"How can they still be there when I'm dead inside, April? They were part of my life before, but now I'm—"

"You're here," she told him, and held her hand to his chest. His heartbeat was strong and sure under her palm. "With me. Now."

"You make me feel things I'd thought I lost the capacity to feel. You make me want things—" His voice broke off as he drew in another deep breath. He leaned down until their foreheads touched. They stood that way for several long moments, her lips just grazing his. She breathed him in and it felt like she was pulling his essence into her lungs. Like he was part of her. A part she thought she'd lost after the illness and heartbreak that had changed who she was inside.

"I'm sorry I can't be the man you deserve," he whispered. "I'll hurt you and girls. I hurt everyone—"

"Not now." She pressed her mouth to the base of his neck, tasted the salt on his skin and wanted more. "This moment is ours."

He claimed her mouth then, kissed her until the feel and taste of him was all she knew. Everything else burned away in the flame that was her need for him. He pulled her closer, if that was possible. Their tongues tangled and his hands skimmed under the shirt and up her spine, sending tingles as they moved. His kiss was demanding and consuming, and every inch of her body burned for him. For more.

His lips trailed over her jaw and he nipped at the sensitive flesh of her earlobe. "Will you stay?"

The simple question rocked her. How was it that such a longing could have been buried inside her and she'd never guessed? Even at her most in-love-and-alive, she'd never felt anything quite like the force of her desire for Connor. Still, she shook her head. "I have to go back in case the girls need me. If Shay wakes up…"

"I understand," he said, pulling his hands from underneath her shirt.

No, her body screamed. *Don't let him go.*

"Come with me," she told him, lacing her fingers with his.

He stared at her, his eyes unreadable once more. She hated that he could slip behind his mask so easily. She wanted to break through until she saw every bit of him, good and bad. She wanted to *know* him and, in return, allow him access to all the secret places she kept hidden from the rest of the world.

"This isn't real life. We aren't—"

"I don't care." She bit down on her bottom lip. She knew what they were and what they weren't, but now that she'd awakened to her longing, she wasn't willing to abandon her desire so easily. "We're here now. It doesn't need to be more than that. We can agree—"

He squeezed shut his eyes, then looked at her again, his gaze empty. "It's a mistake, April."

"Make it with me, Connor."

She prepared herself for his rejection. Instead, he lifted her hand to his lips, turned it over and placed a tender kiss at the center of her palm. "Are you sure?"

"Right now," she answered honestly, "yes."

For some reason, that made him smile. "You're all sweetness on the outside but you have a core of pure steel."

"Is that a compliment?"

"Right now, yes," he said with a wry grin. "I'm coming with you."

"I'm glad."

As she led him through the smaller cabin, April pointed to the second floor and placed a finger over her lips. Connor was grateful for the sleeping girls because he wasn't sure he could actually form words at this moment.

He'd never expected to be in this place again. Wanting. Needing. The ache he felt for April went beyond the physical. It was elemental, as if in the span of a few short days she'd become a necessary part of him, vital to his very existence.

He'd never believed in a muse, but something about April had given new life to his creativity. He'd written close to a hundred pages in the past two days, and it wasn't the garbage he'd forced onto the page over the previous six months. The drivel that had prompted a call from his editor and a suggestion that he start over on the story. He knew as the words were pouring out of him that they were the best he'd even written.

Every time he thought about the beautiful redhead now leading him up the stairs, his fingers itched for the keyboard again. Not as much as they itched to touch every inch of her delicate skin. To know if it was as creamy everywhere as the places he'd seen and touched. He wanted it all, and he was worried that he might never get enough.

It was stupid since, after the holidays ended, he'd be back to his solitary life. The isolation that had once felt like a refuge now loomed like a dark, desolate wasteland.

But he wouldn't think of that now.

She turned to him in the doorway of the bedroom at the end of the hall. "Well, this is it," she said, tucking a lock of hair behind her ear, then untucking and then retucking. Nervous. She was nervous.

Connor smiled despite himself.

"We're good?"

"Sure." She smiled, crossed her arms over her chest. "Yep. We should…um…I mean I know what to do. It's just…"

He stepped closer, cupped her cheek and kissed her gently. "What's going on, sweetheart? It wasn't that long of a walk across the driveway."

"You're the one who said it was a mistake."

He licked the seam of her lips. "I'm an idiot. Ask Ranie."

She laughed. "That girl likes you. A lot."

"And you, April?" He tugged at the hem of her shirt. "Do you like me?"

"Against my better judgment," she admitted.

He pulled back, searched her deep brown gaze. "Tell me now, April. Is this a mistake?"

"No, but…" She pressed her lush, kiss-swollen lips together. "I haven't been with a man since my husband."

"I haven't been with a woman since my wife."

"You don't understand. I haven't been with a man since my *cancer*." Her arms wrapped tighter around herself. "My *breast* cancer."

She said the words like they were a challenge—as if she expected him to run from the room at the mention of her cancer. The knowledge of what she'd been through shocked him, but he wasn't scared by it. It only made him admire her more. "I'm sorry, April."

She shook her head. "Don't you dare feel sorry for me," she whispered. "I'm a survivor. But it's changed me. It's changed my body."

"I don't feel sorry for you," he clarified. "I'm sorry for anything that caused you pain, but never doubt that you are beautiful." He stepped closer. "*I* think you're beautiful."

"You haven't seen me."

"I've seen the most important parts," he said, leaning in to kiss her forehead. "Your intelligence." He slowly drew one finger down the side of her face, over her neck and collarbone to the center of her chest. "Your beautiful heart." He lowered his mouth to brush against hers. "Although I'm partial to this part of you, as well."

She kissed him back, but her body remained stiff. He took her hands in his and slowly drew her into the room, shutting the door behind them. "Tell me what you want me to know," he said when she sat on the edge of the bed.

She blew out a breath. "The cancer was caught early, so I opted for a lumpectomy and then a course of radiation and chemo as my treatment plan. There's a scar and... I'm not a young girl anymore. My body—"

"Is perfect," he interrupted. "Because it's yours." He pulled his shirt over his head and turned so that his back was to her. He heard her gasp and let his eyes drift closed. "During the accident, my seat belt malfunctioned and I was thrown from the car as it rolled. I landed against the edge of the guardrail."

Her fingers traced the length of his scar. Other than the hospital staff, no one had touched that part of his body. He was surprised to find that the skin there was still sensitive after all this time, or maybe it was simply a reaction to April's touch.

He shifted to look at her and found her eyes bright with unshed tears. "No, April. No crying."

She swiped at her cheeks and nodded. "I haven't dated or been with a man since my divorce because I'm afraid to show anyone that part of me. The physical reminder that I'm not who I was."

"We don't have to—"

She reached for the hem of her pajama top. "I want to, Connor. With you." Her smile was wry. "Even if it's only temporary. I have to start somewhere, right?"

Those words sent a stab of jealousy piercing through him. He had a feeling that once he started with April he would never want to finish. To think of another man with her after he was gone was a sharp pain in his chest. But then she lifted her shirt over her head and let it drop to the floor and all he could say was "Thank you for starting with me."

She wore a pale pink satin bra, the soft color a perfect complement to her creamy skin. His gaze snagged on the jagged edge of an incision he could see above the fabric. At this moment, he wanted to throttle her ex-husband for letting her go and also express his gratitude for the man's stupidity since it allowed Connor the gift of having April here with him.

He wanted so badly to touch her, but forced his hands to remain in his lap. "There's one thing," he said. "I wasn't expecting this and I don't have protection."

A wisp of sadness flitted across her gaze before she smiled. "One benefit to the cancer, I suppose. My treatment sent me into early..." She paused, as if the word was too difficult to say out loud. "I can't get pregnant."

"I'm sorry."

She shrugged. "Some things weren't meant to be."

"This *is* meant to be," he whispered, leaning forward again. He took her mouth, planning to go slowly. But as soon as her tongue touched his, all the desire he'd banked came howling back to life inside him. He needed her now. All of her.

As if she was responsible for the very beat of his heart. As if touching her could somehow sew together all the shattered bits of his soul and make him a whole person again. It was foolish, he knew, and too much to expect of anyone. She had scars of her own, and not just the one on her body.

He'd spent so much time wallowing in his own grief that he'd forgotten how it felt to offer comfort and pleasure to another person. Now he wanted to rediscover that piece of himself. The one that wasn't buried in sorrow. The one that could feel something besides pain and regret.

He forced himself to slow down and savor the moment. Every sigh and moan that escaped April's beautiful mouth. Damn, but he loved her mouth. He kissed her with every part of himself, pulling her closer and then lowering her onto the bed. His fingers found the clasp of her bra and flicked it open. She stiffened as he drew the straps down her arms.

"Beautiful," he murmured as her breasts were revealed to him. He kissed the scar that traveled the edge of one breast as he cupped the other one in his hand. She let out a sound that was half sob and half moan as he gently sucked her nipple into his mouth.

Her hands reached around his back, her fingernails lightly scratching a path over his spine.

"Let me see you," he whispered as he raised his head to look into her eyes. "I want all of you."

She nodded and he stood, flipping down the covers as he did. She backed up onto the sheets and he reached for her pajama bottoms, curling his fingers into the waistband of her panties at the same time. He tugged the material down over her hips, revealing every inch of her to him. She looked at him shyly from beneath her lashes. With her copper hair tumbling over her shoulders and her skin milky white in the early morning light that filtered through the curtains, he was almost brought to his knees. She was the most beautiful thing he'd ever seen. She was long and curvy in all the right places, her body clearly sculpted by the yoga classes she taught.

"You're staring," she said, her mouth curving slightly.

"I could look at you all night."

She laughed, a husky sound that made him want her all the more. "I'd rather you join me." She crooked a finger at him. "Are you waiting for an official invitation?"

He shucked off his pants and boxers, realizing his fingers were trembling as he did, and then climbed onto the bed. He felt like an untried schoolboy with April, excited and nervous and so damn grateful to be exactly where he was. That gratitude was new for him, and he concentrated on that. Focused on making April believe she was as beautiful as the way he saw her.

Her skin was smooth and he skimmed his hands up her legs. "I want to touch you everywhere," he whispered, and pressed a kiss to her belly.

"I don't think I have enough patience for that right now," she said, pulling on his shoulders until he brought his mouth to hers.

"We have time," he said, and deepened the kiss. She wrapped her legs around his hips in a silent invitation that he was happy to accept. Sliding into her was like nothing he'd ever felt. It was as if she'd been made for him, the way she tasted and smelled the perfect combination to stoke his passion even higher. He licked a trail down her neck, sucking lightly when she squirmed. Her fingers kneaded the muscles of his back and she arched into him, moaning when he changed their movements.

"You feel so good," he said.

She whispered his name on a sigh and then opened her eyes to gaze into his. The pressure inside him built and they continued to move together.

"So good," she repeated, and he felt her body stiffen and then tremble around him. Her tiny moans and the flush that colored her cheeks spurred him on and he came inside her, shuddering at the power of his release. She held him and he continued to drop gentle kisses at the base of her throat before scooping her into his arms and turning so that she was sprawled across him.

They lay like that for several minutes and Connor finally felt his heartbeat return to normal. She lifted her head, resting her chin on his chest. He could feel her gaze but wasn't ready to open his eyes. Couldn't risk her seeing what this moment meant to him. He had no intention of changing his plans. This was temporary. A holiday fling.

His stomach tightened, rejecting his brain's intention, but he ignored it. He'd become a master at ignoring his feelings. There was no reason to change now.

"What are you thinking?" she asked softly, and he was struck by the wariness in her tone. How was it possible that this woman could read him so easily?

"No words," he said, schooling his expression as he met her gaze. "There are no words for how amazing that was."

She studied him for a moment before flashing a quick smile. "Even from the writer?"

No words, he wanted to tell her, would keep his

heart safe from being destroyed when this ended. All the ways he didn't want it to end scared the hell out of him so, instead of answering, he kissed her again. As if he could wrench out every bit of pleasure from her and somehow make it enough to allow him to walk away.

Chapter Seven

Connor pressed his fingers to the cold glass the next afternoon as he watched the girls and April play in the small clearing behind the cabin. They were bundled up in parkas, hats and mittens. It had snowed again overnight, and April's bright hair seemed to sparkle against the reflection of the pristine layer of snow enveloping the ground and surrounding trees.

Ranie was on her knees, rolling a ball of snow across the clearing. Shay applauded as the ball, clearly intended to be the base of a snowman, got bigger. She started to shout something to her sister, then clapped a mittened hand over her mouth. April said something he couldn't make out before glancing up at his bedroom window.

Instinctively, he backed out of sight. He hadn't seen her since he'd left her bed late last night. She'd been asleep next to him, her hair fanned out in glorious waves across the pillow. She'd looked so peaceful and content, and he'd wanted to stay wrapped around her all night long. But he was afraid that would send the wrong message about what was between them so had sneaked out, back to the stillness of his own cabin.

Instead of sleeping, he'd sat down in front of his laptop. He'd expected to stare at the blank screen, his frustration mounting until his head was a jumble of anger and disillusionment. But, as had happened over and over in the past few days, his fingers had flown across the keyboard, pumping out words and scenes that had been locked inside him since Margo's and Emmett's deaths. He was so close to the end of the book, and his momentum continued to grow.

It triggered both relief and guilt, because somehow losing his gift had seemed a form of penance for living when his family had perished. It had been inadequate punishment, but it was something.

Now he had his story *and* April. It was almost too much. The unfamiliar happiness that washed through him was both a balm to his sorrow and a jab at the misery that had been his constant companion.

With one last glance out the window, he forced himself to sit back down at the bedroom's rolltop writing desk. He'd sent off an email to his editor early this morning, telling her he'd be delivering the story she was waiting for by the end of his two weeks at the cabin. Now he opened her response, an enthusiastic paragraph about pushing up release dates and a potential media tour. Panic gripped Connor's chest and he slammed shut the laptop screen.

Another happy shout drew him to the window. Although she faced Shay, April pointed at the cabin, her back to him. Connor had a perfect view of Shay's face as her sweet smile faded and she dropped her head to stare at the ground. He could almost hear April's sigh as she bent to wrap her arms around the girl.

In that moment he'd never felt like a bigger ass. Those girls, who had lost so much, couldn't even enjoy a day out in the snow because he'd demanded peace and quiet. The truth was that at the start of his career, before he'd had a home office, he'd often written in bustling coffee shops, proud of his ability to block out background noise as he concentrated. Even after Emmett was born, he'd heard the sounds of baby cries from his desk when Margo came home from work and took over the parenting. There was no reason for him to insist on perfect quiet other than his wolfish agitation at hearing young voices.

But the sounds didn't poke at his sanity the way they had after the accident. At that time, any high-pitched sound reminded him of Emmett and the boy's scream in that last moment before the truck had slammed into their vehicle. It was one of the main reasons Connor had become such a hermit. He was afraid of being swallowed by panic and not having the ability to snap himself out of it. But he'd grown weary of giving his demons so much power.

He hurried down the stairs, shrugging into his coat as he grabbed a pair of gloves and knit cap from the storage bench by the back door. The sunshine bouncing off the snow had him squinting, and he took a pair of sunglasses from his coat pocket and slid them on. April and both girls looked up as he rounded the corner to the back of the house.

April moved toward him quickly, her thick boots crunching in the snow. She held out her hands as if to physically stop him. "It was just a little shout," she said, her voice pitched low. "It's hard to stay quiet when you're five, but she's trying."

He looked over her shoulder to the girls. Ranie had come to stand next to Shay, her arm wrapped protectively around her sister's shoulders. The older girl glared at Connor as Shay chewed on her bottom lip. He realized he hadn't seen the girls since he'd fled after their trip to town and now they expected he was here to complain and yell.

Great. *Now* he felt like a bigger ass.

"I've come to help," he said quickly.

April blinked like he was speaking a foreign language.

"With the snowman," he clarified.

"Did you fall and hit your head sneaking away last night?"

"I didn't sneak away," he said through clenched teeth. "You were asleep."

She poked him in the chest. "Because you *snuck* out of bed without waking me."

He took off one glove and tapped his finger to the tip of her cold nose. She drew away, making him smile. "You're beautiful when you're angry, but not as beautiful as you are with your hair spread out over the white sheets and not nearly as lovely as when I was deep in—"

"Okay, girls," April called, whirling away from him but not before he saw the blush coloring her cheeks. "Connor's going to help us with the snowman."

"Do we still have to be quiet?" Shay asked, continuing to nibble on her lip.

April glanced over her shoulder, one brow arched. If eyebrows could speak, hers would be saying, *See what a jackass you are*. But he didn't need her to enlighten him.

He shook his head, moving toward the girls. "You can be as loud as you want," he said, crouching in front of Shay. "I've gotten a lot of writing done this week and I appreciate how you've helped me. Things are going well enough that I can take a break, and even when I go back to work, you can make noise."

"I don't want to bother you," she said quietly.

"You don't, sweet girl. How's that baby kitten?"

Shay's face immediately lit with pleasure. "He drinks from a bottle and sleeps with me and Ranie. We're going to bake cookies after the snowman. You can help and then you'll see him."

"He doesn't want to bake cookies," Ranie muttered.

"Do I get to lick the batter bowl if I help?"

Shay nodded. "Yep. We each get a spoon. At least that's how Mommy did it."

"Sounds like a plan to me," April said from where she stood a few feet away.

Connor straightened. "Are you better at making snowmen than ice skating?" he asked, sliding a glance at Ranie.

Her mouth dropped open. "I was great at ice skating."

He shrugged. "With some coaching. You need help with Frosty?"

"I can roll a way bigger snowman than you."

"We'll see about that," he said with a grin. "How

about a wager? Whoever builds the biggest snowman gets first dibs at the batter bowl?"

Shay giggled. "Ranie loves cookie dough."

He pointed at the older girl. "Then you'd better get rolling."

"You're on," she said, returning his smile before she took off for the corner of the clearing where the snow was deepest.

Connor turned to April.

"How do you do that?" she asked. "Make things good with her so easily? Other than when she's holding that cat, I can barely get her to crack a smile."

He leaned in close. "Maybe I have a gift with words *and* prickly women."

"I am *not* prickly," she protested.

"I know. You're perfect." He glanced over to make sure Ranie and Shay were busy, then brushed his mouth across April's. She tasted like cold and mint, and he wanted nothing more than to wrap his arms around her until she was warm and pliant under him. "I didn't sneak away," he said as he reluctantly pulled back.

She gave a delicate snort.

"I walked away quietly," he added, earning a small smile.

"You're good when you make an effort."

"I'm going to make more of an effort." He leaned in again. "Later tonight."

This time she laughed for real, and it was more rewarding than any glowing review of his books.

"April, will you help me find a nose for Ranie's snowman?" Shay called. "We're helping her beat Connor."

April reached down, grabbed a handful of snow and

threw it directly at his face. "You'd better get rolling," she said, and ran off to join the girls.

His demons were silent as he watched her go. She was the only thing he'd found that could effortlessly keep them at bay. They were no match for the joy she brought to his slowly brightening life.

With a tremor of unfamiliar hope unfurling inside him, he bent to the ground and started rolling.

"You know there are carbs in that pizza crust." April nudged Connor as he helped himself to another slice later that night.

"What's a carb?" Shay asked, wiping her hand across her mouth.

"Napkin," April said at the same time as Connor, and then slanted him a small smile.

Shay bounced up and down in her seat. "Jinx," she called out. "You owe each other a soda."

April had no idea what she was talking about, but Connor answered, "The jinx machine is out of order. Please insert another quarter."

Ranie rolled her eyes, but Shay's gaze widened. "How do you know about jinx?"

Connor took a breath. "My son loved getting jinxed," he said after a moment.

Shay nodded. "I wish I could have met him. I don't have many friends my age."

"He would have been eight next month." Connor placed the piece of pizza back on his plate. "But he loved playing with kids of all different ages. I'm sure you would have been good friends."

Silence descended for a moment and then Ranie pushed away her chair from the table. "Shay, let's clear our plates and I'll show you that new app I downloaded on my iPad."

The younger girl lifted her hand to her mouth. She reached for her napkin and wiped it across her lips. "I'm sorry you're really bad at making snowmen," she said to Connor, and then followed Ranie to the kitchen.

April tried to hide her smile as Connor turned to her.

"Really bad?" he asked.

"Pretty awful," she told him.

"He was just a little off-center. It gave him character."

"His head fell off before you'd taken two steps away."

"Maybe," he admitted, "making snowmen isn't one of my gifts."

She rested her head on his shoulder. "You have others."

He pointed to the two empty seats across from them. "I can sure clear a room."

"Is it difficult to talk about your son?"

He took so long to answer she wasn't sure he was going to. Then he said, "To some people, but not Shay. She's so matter-of-fact about it. Most of my friends and family either tiptoe around the subject or immediately start to cry when they see me. After the accident, Margo's mom would call me every day to tell me details of Margo's life when she was a girl." He closed his eyes for a moment, the soft Southern drawl of his mother-in-law's voice echoing in his mind. "Some of the stories I'd heard before, but the constant barrage of details when I was already so broken…" He opened his eyes again, met her gaze as she tipped her head to look at him. "I stopped taking her calls. I turned off my machine. I couldn't…"

"It's okay."

He shook his head. "Her parents were as heart-broken as me. They lost their only daughter. I didn't protect my family. I was too weak—"

"I read more reports about the accident on the internet," April told him. She felt him stiffen. "You couldn't have done anything."

"I could have gotten them out of the car before it caught on fire. I was too fat and out of shape to move when it mattered." He pushed the abandoned plate toward the center of the table. "It's why I got healthy. No carbs. Lots of protein and exercise. I won't ever fail someone I love again." He gave a gruff laugh that broke her heart a little. "Of course, there's no one left alive who I love."

Another jab to her heart. Of course she didn't expect him to love her. Of course she wasn't falling in love with him. She'd barely known him for a week. They'd spent one night together. Maybe it was the best night of her life, but that didn't matter.

Her heartache was insignificant compared to how his had been broken, but she was too raw to offer him any comfort right now. Instead, she pasted a bright smile on her face. "So the pizza was a pretty big deal?"

"Don't forget the cookies."

"You inhaled a half dozen."

There was a rustling under the table and then a black ball of fluff clawed at her pant leg. Jingle jumped into her lap.

"He looks good. I think he's grown in the past few days."

"He makes them really happy," she said, "and it's going to be terrible when they have to give him back."

"Maybe they won't."

"There's no way Jill's sister will let them keep a kitten."

"April," he said softly. "Those girls belong with you."

"No." She jumped up from her chair, dropping the kitten onto the table as she did. Ignoring the sudden trembling in her fingers, she collected the pizza stone and both their plates. "That's not an option, Connor."

"Why?"

"Does it matter?" She stalked over to the kitchen sink and dumped the plates and pizza stone into it. She went to open the dishwasher, but Connor was next to her, blocking the door. "You don't get to do this," she said.

"Why?" he asked again, and she couldn't tell whether he was repeating his question or wondering about her anger. She opened herself, gave her temper free rein in a way she normally wouldn't. She'd learned early on to control what she felt until her optimism had become an inherent part of her. Yoga helped with that. Whenever she felt pressure building, she'd go through her favorite restorative sequences until her equilibrium returned.

But she had no center of balance with Connor. She was like his snowman, continuously off-center and on the verge of toppling over.

She gave him a small push and he backed up a step, far enough that she could open the dishwasher. Flipping on the faucet, she rinsed the plates and began to load them. "You wrap yourself in your tragedy like it's a warm blanket. It's defined you, and anytime you're uncomfortable you pull it up to your chin like a protective layer. You don't get to hide behind your demons and still demand that I put aside mine. I honor what you've been through and how it's shaped you, Connor."

"You've pushed me every day since you showed up at that cabin," he answered, but there was no anger in his tone.

She lifted her gaze to his, and his green eyes were lit with understanding. She didn't want understanding. She was baiting him because his anger would mute the other emotions tumbling through her.

"It's not the same."

"Those girls need a family, April. They need you."

She almost laughed at that. Because if anyone was needy in this scenario, it was her. All the need and desire she'd locked away was now pushing on the door of her heart. She could feel the barricades starting to crumble and was working overtime to shore up the cracks in her armor. That involved not allowing herself to even entertain the idea of keeping Ranie and Shay.

"I'm not a good bet for them," she said, drying her hands on a dish towel and then slamming shut the dishwasher. "Their mother died and if my cancer returns…"

"You can't live your life letting the fear of a future that may never happen run it."

"Watch me."

"You'd be good for them," he said softly.

She shook her head. "I'm not good for anyone." No matter how much she tried, how much she gave to her friends and the Crimson community, her deepest secret was that it was all a mask. Everything she did was to prove that she added value and was worthy of the love and friendship people offered her. Because she didn't believe she was worthy of it just for being who she was.

He reached for her, pulled her close and wrapped

his arms around her. She tried to stay stiff, to ignore how right it felt to be surrounded by the strength and heat of him.

"We're quite a pair," he whispered, and all the effort she'd made to fortify her defenses didn't matter. They fell away in an instant, as if he'd snapped his fingers and worked some kind of strange, desperate magic. She sagged into him and let him support her. All her tarnished edges and dusty corners. She didn't hide anything, only pulled air in and out, matching her breathing to the steady rhythm of his heartbeat.

"You're making an effort," she whispered after a long minute. "That counts."

"You're giving those girls a Christmas they won't forget," he answered. "And dragging me along for the fun. That counts, too."

She sniffed. "I'm not dragging you—"

He cut off her words with a gentle kiss. "Thank you," he said. "For being you."

"April?"

Shay's voice was uncertain. April pulled away from Connor and turned to where the girl stood in the kitchen doorway, a book held to her stomach.

"Are you ready for the story?" she asked.

Shay nodded, then her blue gaze flicked to Connor. "I was wondering if Connor would read it to us tonight?"

Oh, dear. April supposed she didn't need to push Connor when Shay was around. That sweet girl was determined to bring him back to life. She smiled at him over her shoulder. "Each night leading up to Christmas we read a different story out of the Christmas book bought the other day. They're short but if…"

"Dragging me," he whispered, "in the best way possible."

He stepped around her toward Shay. "It just so happens that in addition to my mad skills making snowmen, I'm a master story reader."

Ranie had come to stand next to her sister. "This should be a treat," she muttered, but a smile lit her eyes.

"Can we have cookies while we listen?" Shay asked April.

April nodded. "One more each. You get settled on the couch with Connor and I'll put them on a plate."

Her cell phone rang as she turned for the counter, and she recognized Sara's number. "Are you checking up on me from paradise?" she asked as she accepted the call.

Sara's throaty chuckle sounded through the phone. "I'm having a margarita in your honor."

"I don't drink margaritas," April answered with a smile.

Sara laughed again. "You should, my friend. You should."

"How's vacation and why are you calling? Is everything okay at Crimson Ranch?"

"It's fine and vacation is perfect. I should try it more often."

"You'd get bored and bug that handsome husband of yours," April told her.

"Oh, I'm *bugging* the heck out of him on this trip. He's not complaining." Sara sounded happy and relaxed, and April was glad for her. "I wanted to check in on our cabin guest. Connor's editor called to thank me. She said he's going to finish his book during this trip. Apparently, the studio that made the first movie is interested in film rights. I don't know what you've been doing, April, but as usual you've got the magic touch with difficult guests."

"He's not too bad," she said quietly, glancing at the doorway that led to the cabin's small hearth room.

"Really? I heard he went off the deep end after he lost his wife and son, and now he's a total antisocial hermit."

"April, come on." Shay ran into the room and skidded to a stop in front of her.

April fumbled for the mute button on her phone but ended up holding her fingers over the microphone.

"Connor and Ranie are having a pillow fight and you need to referee." The girl was bursting with excitement and shouting at the top of her lungs. "Bring the cookies to distract them."

She held a finger over her lips and whispered, "I'll be there in a minute. Don't run in the house."

Shay heaved the impatient sigh of a five-year-old, and then turned and sprinted back out of the room. "April's got the cookies," she yelled, her voice carrying even after she'd disappeared.

"Sara, I need to go. Have a—"

"You're kidding, right?" Her friend sounded stunned. "You can't hang up without an explanation. Pillow fights and cookies? Who is Ranie? And is there a child at the cabin?"

April made a pathetic attempt at white noise. "Sorry, Sara, you're breaking up."

"You can't pawn me off with fake static. What's going on, April?"

April sighed, pressed a hand to her forehead. She hadn't drunk more than an occasional glass of wine since her cancer diagnosis, but this was a moment she could have used a shot of hard liquor. For medicinal purposes, of course. "It's under control. You have to trust me."

"Of course I trust you." Sara's voice gentled. "But I need to know you're okay. I know how you take on more than you should because you can't say no. The point of being up on the mountain with a hermit was that you'd have time to relax, too. Whatever is going on there—"

"I'm fine," April lied. "Everything is fine."

Shay yelled for her again.

"I need to go. Enjoy your vacation and I'll talk to you when you're back in town."

"If you need anything," Sara said quickly, "call me. Anytime. Take care of yourself, April."

"I will." The lie stuck in her throat. She swallowed, then made her voice bright. "Merry Christmas, Sara. Give Josh a hug for me and I'll see you in the New Year."

"Merry Christmas" was the last thing she heard her friend say before ending the call.

Everything might not be fine, but that was her own fault. She'd let her heart get involved with the three people waiting for her in the next room. They meant something to her, different from what she'd expected and more than she could handle without being hurt. But she'd committed to doing her best to heal those girls and Connor. No matter what life had thrown at her, April had always believed Christmas was a time of magic. She wasn't going to give up on that now.

The sound of raucous laughter spilled from the hearth room into the kitchen. Laughter was a good reminder of how far they'd come in just a few days. She plated the warm cookies and, humming a holiday tune under her breath, moved toward the happy sounds.

Chapter Eight

A loud crash from downstairs made Connor jerk away from his keyboard. He glanced over his shoulder at the closed bedroom door. Was April trying to get his attention?

It seemed unlikely since she'd been avoiding him all day. Maybe she was angry again that he hadn't spent the whole night with her, but he'd made a point of waking her before he'd crawled out of her bed around midnight. She'd given him a sleepy kiss and a smile before falling back to sleep. He'd assumed that meant she was okay with him leaving. The truth was, even if he'd wanted to stay, the words were pounding through his brain at such a fever pitch he couldn't sleep. He'd returned to his cabin and stayed at the computer until the sky had turned pink and orange with the dawning of a new day.

Only then had he forced himself to rest for a few hours before heading down to the treadmill in the basement. He'd timed his workout so he might see April making breakfast, but she hadn't made an appearance all morning. It was easy enough for him to fry a couple eggs, and he'd had a small stab of guilt at the fact that he was sleeping with a woman who, in a roundabout way, worked for him. Maybe he should make her breakfast? Or dinner. He'd checked the refrigerator and pantry and figured he could whip together some sort of decent meal for her and the girls.

He'd been the one to cook most of the meals when Margo was at work, and he expected the thought of cooking for someone else to feel uncomfortable. Instead, he liked the idea of doing his part for the woman who had already done so much for him.

But April hadn't come to the house at lunch and the small cabin next door had remained quiet all day. He could have texted her, but something had stopped him. Maybe there was another reason she was staying away. Maybe he'd shown her too much of himself, and it was more than she was willing to take on. He wouldn't blame her, even as disappointment coiled around his gut.

Anger rose to the surface, sharp and familiar. She *did* work for him. Even if she'd decided she wanted nothing more to do with him, she still had a job. He stalked toward the stairs, letting the demons he'd kept under lock and key have free rein inside him. They stretched and yawned, then gnashed their teeth, prepping for a fight he didn't exactly want but couldn't seem to stop himself from seeking.

He came up short as he turned the corner for the

kitchen. Ranie was on her knees with a towel, wiping up what looked to be enough water to fill a bathtub. Shay stood on a chair pulled to the counter chopping carrots with…damn, was that a butcher knife in her hand? April was nowhere in sight.

"Hey, girls," he said softly, not wanting to startle a five-year-old wielding an eight-inch knife. "What's going on?"

Ranie froze on the floor, glancing up at him.

Shay turned and the look in her eyes wrecked him. "We're making you dinner," she said with a hitch in her voice. "But you don't have any food in the cabinets. Ranie's real good at noodles or mac n' cheese. You only…"

"Sweetheart," he said, stepping closer. "Put the knife on the counter."

Ranie straightened and, after moving behind Shay, grabbed the knife out of her sister's hand.

"We'll figure out something," the older girl told him, her chin tipped up. "You have eggs. I can make eggs. Go back to whatever you were doing and—"

"Why are you two making dinner?"

"We want to," Ranie said. At the same time Shay whispered, "April's sick."

Ranie nudged the girl's shoulder. "Be quiet, Shay."

Connor's mind raced and spun as he tried to assimilate the scene before him and the little girl's words. "What do you mean she's sick? Is she at the other cabin still? What's wrong?"

The two sisters looked at each other, an entire silent conversation occurring before his eyes.

"I'll see for myself," he said, already turning and heading for the door. He shoved his feet into boots and was shrugging into his coat when the girls came rushing after him.

"No." Ranie shouted that one word into the silence.

Connor stopped, his hand on the doorknob. "Tell me what's going on."

"She says it's just a stomach bug." Ranie dropped her gaze, wrapping her thin arms around herself. "She doesn't want you to see her right now."

"She's *really* sick," Shay whispered, and looked so miserable that Connor instinctively opened his arms. With a muffled sob she ran into them and he lifted her against his chest, her weight insubstantial and yet unsettling as her shoulders shook and she cried into his shirt.

He murmured soothing words into her hair. She smelled like sugar and sweat and child. A universal scent that wrapped around his soul, tugging tendrils of memory from their hiding place. His demons quieted, as if lulled by her nearness, watching and waiting to see what would happen next.

Ranie took a step closer and put a soft hand on her sister's back. "Our mom threw up a lot during that last round of treatment. It upsets Shay and..." She clamped her mouth shut, her blue eyes frightened and so big against her pale skin.

"It's going to be okay," he said, and opened his embrace to include her. She allowed herself to be held for only a few moments before pulling away. Shay still clung to him, though, and Connor found that he didn't want to let go of her. He shifted her in his arms so he could hold her as he walked and then led the two girls across the driveway to the smaller cabin.

He held open the front door for Ranie. "When did it start?"

"I guess in the middle of the night," Ranie admitted reluctantly. "She was sick when we woke up this morning."

He started to ask why she wouldn't want the girls to tell him but wasn't sure he wanted to know the answer to that question. April was comfortable being the one to take care of those around her, but what if it was more than that? What if she didn't trust him?

After all he'd shared with her about his weakness and failing his family, she didn't have much reason to have faith in him. But, damn, if he didn't want her to.

He lowered Shay from his arms at the bottom of the staircase. "You two pack your bags while I check on April."

Both girls gave him a look of such horror the ice spikes of guilt hammered into his gut. Apparently, one day of fun in the snow wasn't enough to balance how he'd treated them when they'd first arrived. These girls did not trust him.

"Everyone is moving into the main cabin so I can take care of April," he said gently. "So I can take care of all of you."

Shay nodded and Ranie let out a shaky breath. He could almost see the weight lift from her shoulders. Connor cursed the heavy burden of responsibility this girl had been forced to carry when she should have been focused on being a kid.

"Jingle can come, too, right?" Shay asked. The tiny animal peeked his head around the corner from the hallway.

"Put him in the carrier and bring him along. Once we get April settled, I'll come back for his supplies."

"I can hold him," Shay protested. "He doesn't like the carrier."

Connor shook his head. "I don't have time to chase a kitten through the snow. He can have free rein in the cabin, but he has to make the trip in his carrier."

"Fine," she muttered.

Ranie patted her shoulder. "You get Jingle, and I'll start packing."

As Shay took off down the hall toward the kitchen, Ranie met Connor's gaze. "Thank you," she whispered, her eyes darting toward the cabin's second floor.

"Everything is going to be okay," he told her, and once she'd disappeared after her sister, he headed up the stairs.

He heard the telltale sound of violent retching before he even opened the bedroom door. The bed was empty so he moved toward the bathroom. She was kneeling on the tile floor, hanging on to the side of the toilet as if she was having trouble staying upright.

She stiffened as he crouched behind her and gathered her thick hair into his hands and away from her face. A moan escaped her lips in between heaves, whether from what was going on inside her body or his presence, he couldn't tell. He guessed the latter.

His suspicion was confirmed when she stilled a few minutes later, shallow trembles the only thing racking her body.

"Go," she whispered, her voice hoarse and shaking. "Don't need you."

To prove her point, she shifted away from him like

she was going to stand but crumpled into a heap after just one step.

"Ah, sweetheart," he murmured. "You might not need me, but I'm going to lose my mind if you won't let me help you right now."

Her only response was a soft groan.

He knelt beside her, rubbing his palm over her back. "Let me help you."

She shook her head, her mass of copper hair dull and tangled as it draped over her face, hiding her from his view. Counting on her body's current frailty to prevent a fight, he took her shoulders and eased her around so he could see her face.

Damn. He stifled a gasp at the sight of her sallow skin and chapped lips, the shadows bruising the sunken hollows of her eyes. She didn't look at him and her body was so limp in his arms he couldn't tell if she was still awake. He traced the blue veins of her eyelids with his thumbs.

She stirred as he drew the washcloth over her forehead and cheeks.

"Stomach bug," she croaked out. "Leave me—"

"I'm taking you to my cabin," he told her, surprised when she gathered the strength to fight him. Her skin was burning, and he figured she was half-delusional, thanks to the fever. Although she flailed, there was no strength in the movements and he easily subdued her, gathering her closer. He hoped to heaven this was only a stomach bug. The thought that it might be something more serious made it hard to draw air into his lungs.

"We're going to give it one night," he said as he stood, cradling her in his arms. "Then I'm bringing in a doctor."

"No doctor," she whispered, her body going rigid again. Then she sighed and sagged against him, her breath raspy on his neck.

He headed for the door and found Ranie waiting in the hallway. "She's in bad shape," the girl said, and it wasn't difficult to read the panic in her gaze.

"We'll take care of her," he said with a confidence he didn't feel. Maybe he should call a doctor right away or at least contact someone from Crimson Ranch to let them know what was going on.

As if reading his thoughts, April struggled in his arms. "No," she groaned in a croaky voice that was and wasn't hers.

He didn't answer her as he maneuvered down the hallway. Because even if it was only a virus, no one should trust him with the responsibility of nursing another person back to health. He'd already proved that he couldn't take care of someone who was important to him.

The revelation of his feelings for her had his knees starting to buckle before he clamped down the lid on his emotions. The constant refrain he'd told himself in the past few days...this is a fling, she doesn't matter...held no weight in his heart as the girls led their silent parade through the frozen afternoon air to the other cabin.

Even if what between them ended, April was his. She was in his heart, part of his very makeup. She'd breathed life back into him when he'd thought it was impossible. Stomach flu or something else, he was going to take care of her. He was going to prove that she could depend on him.

The next few days passed in a fevered haze for April. She slipped in and out of sleep as her body seemed to turn in on itself. Even during the cancer treatments, the surgery and the searing pain of recovery, she'd remained conscious of each moment.

Whatever was ravaging her body now had taken it over completely. There were short bursts of lucidity and she clung to those and the details of life swirling around her.

Connor holding her hand. The feel of a cool cloth against her forehead. Struggling to the bathroom or heaving over the bucket at the side of the bed. A girl's voice softly singing Christmas carols. The downy feel of a kitten's fur against her neck. An unfamiliar presence in the room. A doctor?

She'd protested the clinical hands on her, the cold metal of a stethoscope and a pinpoint of light shone in her eyes. Then Connor's strong hands soothing her. A glass of water tipped to her dry lips.

Now she blinked open her eyes, the raw ache in her throat propelling her awake. She felt as if she'd crawled her way through a hot, dark desert, pulling sand into her lungs until they were filled with an abrasive scrape.

A rustling across the room and Connor was beside her.

"Hello, sweetheart," he murmured, and she had the random thought that no one had ever called her that before. Desperately she wanted to be someone's sweetheart. This man's sweetheart.

But not as desperately as she needed a drink.

"Water," she whispered.

He held a glass to her lips and, while swallowing made her wince, it was a cool balm over the fire that burned her throat.

She glanced up at him from under her lashes and

other memories poured into her mind, like a thick soup that meant to choke her. Memories of waking from terrible dreams, the kind that had plagued her during her radiation and chemo, and being comforted in Connor's embrace. Embarrassment followed quickly. She knew from when Sara had cared for her during her treatment, April had a tendency to talk in her sleep. What had she said in the thrall of the fever? What had she revealed when she'd worked so hard to keep her secret fears hidden?

She coughed a little and Connor moved the glass away, dabbed at her chin with a soft cloth. She'd sworn after the cancer that no one would see her so weak again, and a part of her hated that he'd been forced into the role of playing nursemaid.

Perhaps he didn't mind, but she'd watched the way her husband had changed. The difference between how he had looked at her when she'd been whole and healthy and the disgust and pity in his gaze after her diagnosis.

The thought of Connor seeing her that way was more than she could bear.

Tears clouded her vision before she could stop them and immediately he scooped her into his arms, rocking her back and forth like a father would a child who'd scraped a knee. She knew she should fight, show him she was still strong, but the truth was twofold. She wasn't strong and the comfort of being held was too appealing. She wasn't ready to let him go.

"I'm fine," she said, her voice raspy, and she forced herself to pull away.

He gave a tired laugh. "You scared me."

She scooted back against the headboard, shocked

when her arm muscles protested the work of supporting her as she moved. "I'm sorry."

How many times had she said those words to her husband? *I'm sorry I'm sick. I'm sorry I'm not the woman you married. I'm sorry you don't love me anymore.*

Bitterness filled the emptiness in her belly, making her hunger for more than just food.

"Sweetheart, you have nothing to be sorry about."

That word again. *Sweetheart.* Connor's voice was so gentle. She forced herself to meet his gaze, steeling herself for whatever she'd find there.

The tenderness radiating from him was the last thing she'd expected. Again tears pricked her eyes, but this time she blinked them away.

"How long have I been out?"

"Three days." He ran a hand through his hair, and she realized he looked almost as exhausted as she felt. "The fever broke yesterday, shortly after the doctor was here."

"I said no doctors."

"You said a lot of things," he told her. "That one I ignored. Sara insisted—"

"You called Sara?"

"Right away," he answered matter-of-factly.

"It was a stomach bug."

"April," he said on a sigh. "I haven't ever seen a person that sick from a virus. I wasn't taking any chances." He looked away, out the window with the curtains that were drawn so only a bit of light filtered through.

She bit her lip. He'd watched his wife and son die in that car accident. Of course he'd wanted a doctor to take responsibility for her. She was surprised he hadn't shipped her off to the ER so she'd be out of his hair.

No. That was unfair. Connor wasn't her ex-husband. She couldn't lay the shortcomings of another man at his feet.

"Will you open the curtains?" she asked softly, and he stood to do her bidding. "I'm sorry you were worried. And Sara... I'm surprised she didn't fly back from her trip."

He smiled at her over his shoulder. "You know her well. The doctor who made the house call was her brother-in-law."

April cringed. "Jake Travers drove up the mountain to check on me?"

"Only then did Sara agree to stay on her vacation." The mattress sagged as he sat on the edge of it again. "He gave you three liters of IV fluids but said you should still take it easy."

"I feel awful that everyone was so put out by me. He has a family of his own and—"

He placed a finger over her mouth. "He didn't mind, and his wife—"

"Millie?"

"Yes, Millie. She's called twice to check on you." He pulled his phone out of the pocket of his flannel shirt and smiled at the screen. "It seems like half the town has called or texted for updates on your progress. You have a lot of people who care about you."

"I wish no one knew," she said on a sigh. "I don't want people to think that I'm..."

"Human?" Connor asked, one side of his mouth curved.

"Sick," she whispered.

He frowned. "You were sick, April."

"I mean really sick," she clarified. "Most people know my history and—"

"A stomach virus is different than cancer."

"I know," she mumbled, although feeling weak and dependent on other people was universally awful no matter the reason. "It's difficult for me to not be the one taking care of others." She glanced around at the room she was in, suddenly realizing it wasn't her bedroom. "I'm at the main cabin?"

"It was easier to take care of you here."

"What about the girls?"

"They're here, too. In fact, if you're up for it, I know they'd love to see you awake. Both of them have been worried."

"I didn't want them to tell you I was sick."

He flashed a wry smile. "They told me anyway."

She shook her head. "That was stupid and selfish of me. Those girls shouldn't have to feel responsible for anyone but themselves. After everything they've been through…"

"Don't beat yourself up, April," he said, reaching out to take her hand. "Ranie and Shay care about you. They just wanted you to feel better."

"I don't deserve them," she whispered, her chest squeezing. That was why she couldn't keep them. She didn't deserve that kind of devotion, and her instincts around taking care of herself were twisted. She should never have asked the girls to hide her illness from Connor.

Being sick had affected more than April's body. It messed with her mind, bringing back too many memories of not being able to care for herself or having to rely on her husband during her cancer treatments. That experience had changed her, and while she hated the way it had distorted her view of herself and the world around her, she didn't know how to fix it.

"Hey," he told her, tracing his thumb in circles on her palm. "How about you give yourself a break for a minute?" He leaned forward and pressed a kiss on her forehead so gentle it almost broke her heart. "Let's concentrate on the fact that you're on the mend."

"Three days," she muttered. "That means…it's two days until Christmas Eve."

"Yep."

She gave a little groan. "I don't have anything ready. No tree, no presents. I wanted to go to town once more to buy gifts." Disappointment and guilt warred inside her, both vying for equal measure. "I'd hoped to give the girls a special Christmas with their mom gone. Now, it's ruined."

"Nothing is ruined," he assured her. "The best gift those girls can get is you feeling better."

She nodded, even though she didn't agree. She was no one's best thing. "I'm going to brush my teeth and splash water on my face before I see them."

He stood as she moved her legs from under the covers, then caught her as she stumbled when her feet hit the floor. Her head spun as she realized how truly weak her body was.

"Slow down," he murmured against her hair. "I've got you."

Her nerves bristled at his words, but he only wrapped his arms more tightly around her. After a moment, she let herself sag against him. "Thank you," she whispered. "For taking care of me and the girls. I should have said it earlier, but the stupid virus seems to have taken my manners along with my dignity."

"I'm glad to be the one who was here to look out for you."

She tipped her face to meet his gaze. "Do I even want to know what I said in my sleep?"

He couldn't quite hide his grin. "Probably not, but I got lots of creative story ideas."

She groaned again. "Your book. Oh, Connor. I'm sorry. You're supposed to be working on the book, not holding my hair back while I puke."

"I like your hair," he said as he led her slowly toward the bathroom, "and I brought my laptop into your room to work while you slept. Turns out you're inspiring even when feverish and nauseous."

"I'll remember that." She paused, placed her hand on the door frame. "I'm okay from here."

"Are you sure?" He loosened his hold but didn't quite let her go. "The last thing we need is for you to fall and crack your head open."

"I'm fine. I should make myself something to eat after I see the girls."

"I'll heat up some soup."

"We don't have soup."

"The girls and I made it."

She felt her eyes widen. "You made soup?"

"I found a recipe on Pinterest."

"Oh, no." She swallowed another groan. "You were reduced to searching Pinterest?"

"Ranie set me up with an account."

"Well, thank you. But I can take care of—"

He bent his knees so his gaze was level with hers. "I'm not done taking care of you, April. You might be uncomfortable and you can fight me all you want. I'm not walking away."

She sniffed, swiped her fingers across her cheeks. "I like you better when you're a jerk."

He laughed. "That can't be true."

"It's a lie, but things were simpler when you were a jerk."

"Things were simpler when I was alone, but it didn't make me happy." He tucked her hair behind her ears. "You make me happy." He lifted a strand of her hair and cringed. "Even with dried...something stuck in your hair."

"I'm a mess."

"You'll feel stronger after you eat. I'll get the girls."

By the time she'd washed her face and brushed her teeth, April felt almost human again. She looked like hell, pasty and drawn, and her hair was a dirty, stringy mess around her face. She ran a brush through it and then gathered it into a ponytail.

The girls were waiting quietly next to the bed when she walked out into the bedroom. Ranie held on to Jingle like he was keeping her grounded. Connor stood next to the older girl, Shay clinging to his hand. He must have been an amazing father. The thought made her heart ache for him all over again. For what he'd lost and the capacity for caring he was slowly regaining.

"I'm so glad to see you both," she said, lowering herself onto the bed, then opening her arms. Shay launched herself into them immediately, but Ranie held back.

"Are you sure you're okay?" Ranie asked as the kitten squirmed and jumped onto the bed, sniffing at April before curling into a ball at her side.

April nodded. "I need food and a shower, but I'm fine."

"I'll work on the food," Connor said, and left the room.

April stroked the kitten's silky fur. "I remember this guy keeping me company."

"He's a good boy," Ranie whispered. "He was worried about you."

"You threw up a lot," Shay said quietly, tucked against April's chest.

"I'm sorry if I scared you." April rubbed the little girl's back. "Thank you for taking care of me and for letting Connor know I was sick."

Ranie shifted a bit closer. "You aren't mad about that?"

"No, sweetie. You did exactly the right thing. It was wrong that I didn't tell another adult right away. You shouldn't have had to take care of me."

"It's not a big deal," Ranie whispered, sitting next to April.

April adjusted her hold on Shay so she could wrap an arm around Ranie's shoulders.

"Ranie took care of Mommy," Shay added. "But she never puked as much as you."

April drew in a breath. "I was sick after my treatments, too, but this was different. You both understand that, right? I was sick with a stomach virus, but I'll be healthy again. It isn't like—"

"Mommy felt better for a long time." Shay's voice was painfully matter-of-fact. "Then she got sick again."

"I'm not going to…" She paused and then said, "This had nothing to do with cancer." She wanted to tell the girls she wouldn't get sick again, but how could she make that promise? Yes, it had been more than five years since her diagnosis and the odds were good that she'd be fine. But she lived with the knowledge that her cancer could return at any time. She couldn't commit to Ranie and Shay for the long term. How could she take the chance on these two beautiful girls being forced to watch her battle the same disease that had claimed their mother?

She cleared her throat and pasted a smile on her face. "Tell me about what you've done in the past couple of days."

Shay bounced up and down on her knees. "We baked cinnamon bread and played card games. Connor knows one called poker and I'm really good at it."

"Great," April muttered with a laugh. "He's turning you into a card shark."

"She's got skills," Connor said from the doorway. Shay dropped off her lap and Ranie stood as he carried in a tray. "Although it's a little early to decide on a career as a professional poker player."

"I can't be a poker player." Shay pushed her hair away from her face. "I'm going to be a cancer doctor when I grow up," she told them. "So no one else will get sick."

April swallowed back her emotion and smiled. "Your mom would be proud of you," she whispered. Was there no end to this girl's ability to slay her?

Connor waited for her to get comfortable on the bed and then placed the tray across her lap. It held a steaming bowl of chicken soup, a glass of juice and a piece of toast on a small plate. Her stomach grumbled as the comforting scent of soup hit her.

"Ranie did most of the work," Connor told her.

The older girl shrugged. "I like to cook, and Connor helped."

"I cut vegetables," he said with a laugh. "That's prep work."

"Ranie's going to be on the Cooking Channel," Shay said, bouncing up and down.

April spooned up a bite of soup. She closed her eyes to savor the flavors of garlic and roasted vegetables. The warm broth soothed her chafed throat as she swallowed. "It's delicious," she told the girl, and was rewarded with a wide smile.

"You have your mother's smile," she whispered, and Ranie gave a small nod. "Thank you again," April said, taking all three of them in with her gaze, "for all you've done the past few days. I feel so…" She wouldn't say *loved* even though that was the truth of it. "I feel so lucky."

"Now that you're better," Shay announced, trailing one finger over the edge of the quilt. "You should maybe take a bath. You kind of—"

Ranie clapped a hand over her sister's mouth, but April laughed. "Trust me," she told the girl. "I can smell myself, and that's bad."

Shay grimaced. "Real bad."

"After the soup, it's off to the shower for me."

"Shay, let's go finish our puzzle," Ranie suggested. "And you still need to make your bed and get out of your pajamas."

Shay nodded and then leaned closer to April. "I love you even though you smell."

Without waiting for an answer, she turned and walked out of the room. Ranie rolled her eyes and followed.

April froze with the spoon halfway to her mouth.

"Do you remember what it was like when emotions were that simple?" Connor asked.

April took another bite and a sip of juice before answering. "No," she said softly. "My parents got divorced before I was a year old. I don't think things were ever that simple."

"Emmett loved me like that." He sank down into the chair in the corner of the room, elbows on his knees and head in hands. "It was pure and constant and I didn't appreciate it the way I should have. I took both of them for granted, as if their love was my due because Margo had married me and I was Emmett's father. Like that word meant he was mine forever."

"He should have been," she said, and moved the tray off her lap. She got out of the bed slowly, a hand on the nightstand for balance, but found she was steadier after the soup and juice. "I'm sure they both knew how much you loved them." She came to stand in front of him, reaching out to push the hair off his forehead.

"I wish I'd told them more." He lifted his gaze to look at her. "The fact that Shay can still say the words so easily is a miracle. Especially when…"

April pressed her lips together. "When I'm going to let them go?"

"You don't have to—"

"Please, Connor, don't do this. Not now." She stepped out of reach when he would have pulled her closer. "I'm going to shower."

"Are you strong enough?"

There had been many days during her cancer treatment when she hadn't been strong enough to do more than stare at the ceiling. She wasn't that woman any longer. "I'm fine."

In reality, the shower exhausted her. She hated feeling so weak even though she knew it would pass quickly. By the time she turned off the water, she felt dizzy again. She was mustering the strength to climb out when the shower door opened.

A moment later she was wrapped in a fluffy white towel as strong arms lifted her onto the bathroom tile.

Connor turned her to face him. "Can you stand on your own?"

She gritted her teeth and nodded.

Expression serious, he efficiently dried her body and hair and then helped her into a plush terry-cloth robe. She started to protest as he scooped her into his arms, but he whispered, "Let me take care of you, April. Even if you don't need it, I do."

She did need it and, more importantly, she wanted it more than she'd wanted anything in a long time. He carried her across the bedroom and gently placed her on the bed.

"You changed the sheets?"

A half smile pulled up the corner of his mouth. "I'm full service."

She laughed but it quickly turned into a yawn.

"Rest now," he murmured, tucking the blanket and quilt around her. "The girls and I will be here when you wake up."

Even if she'd wanted to argue, her eyelids were too heavy. She drifted off to sleep feeling more cherished than she had a right to.

Chapter Nine

The sound of muffled voices greeted April when she woke again. The muted light coming through the window told her it was late afternoon. She must have slept for hours. She swallowed and stretched, finally feeling on her way to normal.

She realized the voices weren't speaking. They were singing Christmas carols. Climbing out of bed, she retied the sash of the robe and stepped toward the window. This bedroom faced the front of the cabin, and she could see Connor, Ranie and Shay dragging a sled with a pine tree tied to it up the driveway.

Connor was doing most of the hauling, an ax slung over one shoulder. Every few feet Ranie adjusted the tree when it started to drag while Shay skipped next to him, singing at the top of her lungs. All three of them were singing, Ranie's soft voice complementing Shay's enthusiastic soprano while Connor sang harmony. It was the most mangled and adorable version of "Joy to the World" April had ever heard.

They'd cut down a Christmas tree from the forest. The three of them were engaging in a Christmas ritual without her involvement. And…she watched a few more seconds…they all appeared to be having a great time.

Her suitcase was sitting next to the dresser, and she quickly put on sweatpants and a roll-necked sweater before making her way downstairs.

Connor was heaving the tree through the door. "Can I help?" she called from the bottom of the stairs.

He turned, his cheeks flushed with cold, and gave her a wide grin. "You look beautiful," he said, and she felt a blush color her own cheeks.

Shay ran toward her, wrapping cold arms around her waist for a tight hug. "She doesn't smell bad anymore."

Ranie was the only one who looked doubtful. "Are you sure you should be out of bed? What if you have a relapse?"

"It was a virus," April told her gently. "I'll be good as new by tomorrow morning. In fact, I feel fantastic now."

"Okay, then. Good." Ranie's shoulders dropped an inch, as if releasing the tension that had held them so tall.

"You can help us decorate," Shay cried happily. "Will you make hot chocolate? Connor burns it."

"One time," he protested, moving closer until he stood in front of April. "I burned it one time."

Shay shared a look with her sister.

Connor threw up his hands. "What?"

"You make really bad hot chocolate," Ranie said with a grin.

April raised her brows. "How can you mess up cocoa?"

"Let's talk about my chicken soup again."

"You said Ranie did the work on that."

He made a face. "After plenty of debate, we found the perfect Christmas tree."

Shay jumped up and down. "I picked it."

Connor grabbed her and lifted her up high. "I cut it."

April glanced at Ranie, who sighed. "I supervised."

"Come on, Ranie," Shay said when Connor deposited her on the ground again. "Let's open the box of ornaments." The girls laced fingers and headed into the family room.

"Ornaments?" April asked.

"The girls found Christmas decorations in the basement storage room," Connor explained. "We thought it would be a nice surprise for you."

Heat spread through her, and she crossed her arms over her chest to curb the urge to launch herself at him. She'd always loved Christmas, but having these three to share it with made the holiday even more special. It was funny, but a few days in this cabin and it felt more like a home to her than anyplace else on earth.

"You really are beautiful," he whispered, leaning in to brush a soft kiss across her lips. He smelled like cold and pine, but his mouth was warm and soft on hers.

"I look like I've spent three days puking my brains out," she said with a laugh.

He smiled against her mouth. "Your hair is clean."

"Quite an accomplishment."

He pulled back and glanced over his shoulder. "I

need to carry the tree into the family room. There was a tree stand in one of the boxes, so they must have expected someone would celebrate the holidays here."

"More like leftovers from Crimson Ranch. They weren't planning on guests at Cloud Cabin. You were important enough for an exception."

He turned and hefted the tree onto his shoulder. "More like my editor was desperate for me to finish the book."

"And?" she asked, leading the way into the family room.

"I'm close," he told her, and she could hear the pride in his voice. It was so different from how he'd sounded that first day in the kitchen, and she was grateful to be a part of the change in him over the past week. She only hoped it would last even after he returned to his life away from Colorado.

Ask him to stay.

She stopped as the thought popped into her mind, leveling her with its intensity, and was immediately prodded in the back with the tip of a pine tree.

"Sorry," Connor said, his voice muffled under the weight of the tree.

"My fault." She quickly moved into the family room and fisted her trembling hands together. Connor Pierce was a client, nothing more. Maybe more, but not a man she could plan a future around. He'd made it clear he had no room in his heart for anyone other than his wife and son.

April didn't believe that for a second, but he did and she had to honor it.

She raised her eyes and felt a gasp escape her lips. The cabin's cozy family room had been transformed into a holiday wonderland. Stockings dangled from the rough-hewn wood mantel while snowmen figurines and nutcrackers were displayed on the bookcase. There were bright and festive throw pillows decorating the sofa and leather club chairs and, in the corner, a space had been made for the tree. A clear tub of ornaments sat next to the metal tree stand, strands of lights piled on the lid.

"I love it," she said, tears filling her eyes.

"Then why are you crying?" Shay asked, coming over to wrap her arms around April's waist.

"They're happy tears," April told her, running a hand over the girl's soft hair. Connor propped the tree against the wall and grinned at her.

"I only have happy smiles," Shay announced.

"Your smile makes me happy, too." April met Ranie's bright blue gaze and then Connor's piercing green eyes. "Thank you for doing this. It means a lot to me."

Pink tinged Ranie's cheeks. "It wasn't a big deal. We were kind of bored anyway."

Connor nudged her. "You just didn't want to lose to your sister and me at poker again."

The girl visibly relaxed at his gentle teasing. "You should stop corrupting me," she muttered. "I'm an innocent kid."

"Come on, kid," he said, "and help me get this tree in the stand."

When April stepped forward, he shook his head and pointed to the couch. "Sit down until we're ready for ornaments. You still need to take it easy."

"Have you always been so bossy?"

"Not at all," he told her with a wink. "You bring it out in me."

Shay took April's hand and led her to the leather sofa. The family room was a bigger version of the one in the caretaker's cabin. The walls were painted a warm gray and the river-rock fireplace surround went all the way to the vaulted ceiling, giving the room the feeling of a true mountain lodge. The furniture, while new, was overstuffed and comfortable, as if it had been part of the cabin for years. Thick rugs covered the hardwood floors, and both the coffee table and the end table had been built from reclaimed wood.

"I don't know how to put up a Christmas tree," Ranie said, her arms still folded over her chest.

Connor bent to adjust the tree stand. "I'm going to lift the tree. Your job is to guide it into the stand." At Ranie's dubious look, he grinned. "Trust me, you've got this. You're my Christmas wingman."

No, April wouldn't ask him to stay. But her heart would go with him when he left. She couldn't resist this man who thought he had nothing left to give but continued to break through the walls of a fragile girl as if it were the most natural thing in the world. April had started these two weeks thinking she'd be the one to save these three, but it was Connor who had made the biggest difference. She loved him for it, for the effort he was making and how he made her feel. For the man he used to be and the one he was rediscovering inside himself.

No, she wouldn't tell him any of that. Instead, she held the knowledge close to her heart, letting the golden light of it warm her and give her strength.

Within a few minutes they had the tree up and the fasteners tightened around its base.

"Just in the nick of time," she said as Jingle darted into the room and headed for the tree. The branches rustled as the kitten climbed and then poked out his head from midtree height.

"He's our first ornament," Shay said, clapping her hands.

"That cat is a menace," Connor muttered, but was smiling as he reached in and plucked the small animal out of the branches.

Ranie took the kitten and cradled him in her arms. April said a silent prayer that the girls' aunt would allow them to keep their new pet when they went to live with her in California. Connor's gaze was a thick weight on her, but she avoided it, shifting to pull the tub of ornaments closer. It would hurt too much to see the censure she knew she'd find in his eyes. The silent suggestion that she keep these girls in Colorado with her. She couldn't. Or she wouldn't. Either way, the outcome was the same.

"Lights first," she said, keeping her tone light. Connor placed his hand over hers and squeezed.

He bent closer and dropped a tender kiss on the top of her head. "Let's just enjoy our Christmas together," he whispered. "It's all that matters right now."

The words were somehow both a pardon and an apology. Because she wasn't the only one who was too afraid to change her life. As ashamed as she was at her own weakness, the fact that he could understand and absolve her was a balm to the gaping sore that was her heart. She would hold on to their connection and try to ignore the tendrils of pain waiting to take over when the holidays were through.

Connor sat on the couch in the darkened family room, staring at the lights on the Christmas tree. Ice clinked as he raised the glass of bourbon and sipped, the liquor burning a path down his throat. The last time he'd had a drop of hard alcohol had been a month after the funeral. He'd woken up, head pounding, in a pile of his own vomit, surrounded by empty liquor bottles.

At some point during his drunken blackout, he'd apparently gathered the framed photos his wife had lovingly arranged around their house and smashed the frames and then ripped apart the pictures inside. The images had been saved digitally and could be replaced, but the destruction had pierced something deep in his soul. It was his job, as the one left behind, to cherish Margo and Emmett's memory, not ruin the reminders of the life they'd had.

After that, he'd cleaned up his act and gotten healthy. He'd also sold their home and moved to an apartment in the heart of downtown San Francisco. He'd hoped a new location would help him mend all the broken pieces inside him, but he'd only retreated further into himself, willing to make his body healthy but unable to loosen grief's stranglehold on his heart and mind.

Only April and her girls had been able to manage that.

He heard a rustling in the doorway and looked up to see April walking toward him. The Christmas lights reflected off her long hair, making the copper highlights dance in their glow.

"How are you feeling?" he asked. She'd laughed and smiled as the girls had decorated the tree earlier, snapping pictures with her phone when Connor lifted Shay to place the star on top. But soon after, she'd grown tired. He could tell it frustrated her, but she'd allowed him to tuck her back in bed.

"Embarrassed that you're still having to do the work around here." A line of tension appeared between her eyes. "I'm fine now and hope by tomorrow morning I'll be back to normal. If not, I can call Sara and have her find someone to take over for me."

He sat forward, placed his drink on the coffee table, and then grabbed her hand and pulled her into his lap. "You're not getting rid of me yet," he whispered into the curve of her neck. "We're having Christmas here at the cabin. The four of us."

She sighed, her breath a soft wisp at the base of his throat. "It's not fair—"

At those words, he barked out a laugh. "We both know life isn't fair. We also agree this is our time. Right?"

He felt her nod against him. "I don't like feeling that I'm not contributing."

"You're the glue holding us together," he told her, kissing the edge of her jaw. "You make all of this work."

She pulled back to look him in the eye. Her brown eyes were wide and uncertain. "But I have no idea what I'm doing."

"Most people don't," he said, tracing the delicate skin under her eyes with his thumbs. "They do it anyway."

She smiled at that. "It's close to midnight. What are you doing down here?"

"I finished the book. I sent it to my editor an hour ago."

"Connor, that's excellent." She wrapped her arms around his neck and hugged him. It had been a long time since he'd had good news rewarded with a hug. He was surprised at how much the gesture meant to him. "I'm so proud of you."

He dropped a kiss on her shoulder, inching the soft cotton of her pajama top out of the way. "I wasn't sure I could do it," he admitted. "I never believed in the concept of a muse, but you're the reason for this."

She let out a breathy sigh that made heat pool low in his belly. "No. You're the reason. You wrote the words. This is your accomplishment."

"I'm glad I get to share it with you."

She shifted closer, nipped at the edge of his mouth. "Any ideas on how you want to celebrate?"

"Mmm." He lifted the hem of her shirt and splayed his fingers across her back. "Lots of ideas. Creative ones." He drew back. "But I don't want to go too fast for you."

"I like fast." Her gaze was cloudy with passion, her skin flushed.

Damn, she was so beautiful.

"You're still recovering."

She wiggled her brows. "I like slow, too." She bit down on her lip. "I feel fine, Connor. My body needs to move. I'm stiff and sore from lying in that bed for so long. So I can either bring out my yoga mat for a stretching series or—"

"I can help you move those muscles."

She nodded. "That's my preference." She leaned in close, kissing him in a way that was both an invitation and a demand.

He couldn't think of a better way to celebrate than with April in his bed. He stood, holding her in his arms as he made his way through the house and up the stairs. When her tongue touched his, he almost tripped into the hallway wall.

"Hold that thought," he whispered, pulling away and

concentrating on breathing. The last thing he needed was to bang her into something or make so much noise they woke the girls.

He hurried down the hall into his bedroom, gently nudging shut the door with his heel. "Where were we?" he asked against her mouth.

The kiss resumed and he quickly tugged his shirt over his head and then grabbed the hem of hers. He would never tire of looking at her body. It was like a breathing work of art, and he had every intention of giving it the adoration it deserved.

Unlike the first time they'd been together, he took his time with her, kissing and teasing and enjoying the noises she made, every shiver that he felt across her skin. He held the weight of one breast in his hand, bending to lick the rosy tip. When she moaned, he went to his knees in front of her, trailing kisses down her belly to the waistband of her flannel pants. He pulled them over her hips, his breath catching as each perfect inch of her was revealed.

He touched her, tasted her, and when her legs started to tremble, he scooped her up. Kicking back the covers, he laid her flushed and languid across his bed and was transfixed by her beauty. If the night ended now, he would be content.

Then she opened her eyes and crooked a finger at him. "This party is just getting started," she said, and for the rest of the night they celebrated in the best way possible.

April left Connor sleeping in his bed early the next morning. Although she'd only gotten a few hours of rest, she finally felt back to normal. Better than normal.

She was content in a way that was new and refreshing, and even if the sensation was fleeting she planned to savor it while it lasted.

She was also anxious to get back to a routine. Although Connor might like taking care of her, she wouldn't let herself grow accustomed to it.

After prepping for a breakfast of pancakes and fruit salad and brewing a pot of coffee, she made her way to the small exercise studio in the basement of the cabin. Cloud Cabin might look rustic, but it was set up with all the modern amenities a guest could want. The room was cool, so she adjusted the thermostat before pulling a yoga mat from the shelf and unrolling it.

She moved into her first pose, hands clasped in front of her in prayer position and took several deep, cleansing breaths. With each inhalation she could feel herself growing stronger.

A noise had her whirling toward the door. Ranie stood there watching her, still dressed in her pajama pants and a T-shirt.

"Are you better?" the girl asked. Her tone was casual, but she worried her hands together nervously as she waited for an answer.

"I am, sweetie. I've got breakfast ready to make, but I thought I'd do a little yoga while everyone else was still sleeping. You're welcome to join me."

April had made the offer to Ranie each time she'd started a session of yoga, but the girl had always turned away. This morning she took a hesitant step forward. "I'm not very athletic," she muttered. "I'm always on the C team for sports at school."

"Yoga is a balance between the spiritual and the physical. It can calm your mind at the same time it works your body." She moved to the bookshelf and took out another yoga mat. "The beautiful thing is that anyone can benefit from it."

"In that case, you'd better grab two mats."

At the sight of Connor standing in the doorway, a jolt of awareness went through April. All the things they'd done last night, the ways he'd touched her, came rushing into her mind and she had to look away. When she glanced back, he was grinning as if he knew exactly where her mind had gone. He was wearing a faded T-shirt that fit tightly over the broad planes of his chest and a pair of baggy basketball shorts.

"You do yoga?" Ranie asked doubtfully.

"No. Do you?"

"Yes." Ranie bit on the edge of her fingernail. "I'm starting this morning."

"Me, too."

"Guys don't do yoga," she told him with a sniff.

"Of course they do," April said before Connor could answer. "Both men and women have practiced it for centuries." She rolled out the two mats next to each other a few feet behind hers and then pushed a piece of weight equipment off to the side. "Lots of famous men do yoga. Like Sting."

Connor came to help her move the heavy bar. "We know what he's famous for," he whispered, low enough that Ranie wouldn't hear.

April rolled her eyes, remembering the famous musician's quote from the early nineties when he'd extolled the virtue of tantric sex. She'd just gotten her teaching license then and there'd been a short-term upswing in couples joining the studio where she worked.

"Who's Sting?" Ranie asked, coming to stand on her mat.

Connor turned to her. "You're kidding, right? Tell me you know who the Beatles are."

"Of course." Ranie shrugged. "Mom had one of those cars for a while but decided it wasn't big enough."

He thumped the heel of his hand to his forehead. "For Christmas, little girl, I'm getting you an old-school turntable and a stack of albums."

Ranie flashed a calculating smile. "How about a subscription to Spotify?"

"How about we get started so we're not eating breakfast for lunch?" April stepped onto her mat, then glanced at Ranie. "Sting is a singer. He was in a band called The Police before launching an übersuccessful solo career."

Ranie's expression remained blank. "Never heard of him. Mom only liked country music."

"Never heard of Sting?" Connor asked, clasping a hand to his chest, his tone pleading. "Start the yoga before this girl reduces me to tears."

"There are different schools of yoga. I primarily teach in the Vinyasa tradition, which links your breath to movements. We'll start with sun salutations." The studio was warmer now, or maybe it was Connor's intense gaze on her. She shrugged out of her sweatshirt, leaving her in only a pale yellow athletic tank top over a sports bra.

She moved into the first pose, explaining the purpose and how they should be breathing as they moved. From there they continued with the series, focusing on synchronizing their breath through each one. Despite claiming not to be an athlete, Ranie had a natural grace as she moved her body into each new position.

Connor was another story. He was in shape but, in the way of many men, clearly he hadn't paid any attention to his flexibility. He wobbled as he held downward-facing dog and landed facedown on his mat when he tried to straighten from another position.

Ranie giggled as she watched him, which he didn't seem to mind. April shifted into her role as teacher like slipping into a favorite pair of jeans. One of the best things about teaching was working with new students, helping them find the ease within the effort of the poses and connect the body with each breath.

Almost an hour later she took one last breath, completing the final sequence. "How do you feel?" she asked both Connor and Ranie.

"That was…" As Ranie searched for the right word, April held her breath. Somehow, what this girl thought about the practice April loved mattered on a deep, soul level. After a moment, Ranie smiled. "It was awesome. I could do that every day."

A bubble of pure joy burst in April's chest, sending happiness radiating through her. "You *can* do it every day. Yoga will go with you wherever you are." She gentled her tone, hoping Ranie would accept her next words. "I remember coming to visit your mom when you were just a toddler. We did yoga each morning, and you'd be right there with us. Crescent lunge was your favorite. Every time we turned around, you'd be in that pose."

"Mom had a framed photo of me like that in her bedroom," Ranie said with a nod. "I'm going to go upstairs and get dressed. Shay will be waking soon."

"What about you?" April turned to Connor.

"Well," he began, tapping a finger on his chin as if debating. Suddenly he reached out and yanked her into his arms. He kissed her deeply, his hands moving up and down her back, sending shivers of sensation wherever he touched. "I don't know that I'm cut out for yoga, but watching you do it is one of the hottest things I've ever seen."

She laughed against his mouth. "You just liked seeing me bend over."

He pulled away, his green eyes so bright they looked like spring grass after a heavy rain. "That's an added benefit. But you're a natural teacher. The way you worked with both of us and kept things moving and clearly have so much passion for what you do. Why don't you teach classes full-time?"

"Mostly I do," she said, stepping out of his embrace and rolling up the mats. He grabbed the one he'd been using but continued to watch her. "Remember, I'm here as a favor to Sara. But I had to sell my studio in California after my divorce to pay for the medical bills insurance didn't cover. It was another painful reminder of how cancer had changed my life. There was a full year I couldn't do yoga. The very thought of moving into a pose made me sick to my stomach."

His gaze turned solemn. "I get that. You know I get that."

"It was different. Losing your family and losing my business don't even show up on the same radar. I'm embarrassed at how I let the circumstances of my life define who I was." The understanding that she still did that, although it wasn't as obvious from the outside, shamed her. But she didn't think she was strong enough to overcome any more than she already had.

"But now you're teaching again?"

"I started doing classes for the guests at Crimson Ranch. A studio near Aspen asked me to be one of their instructors and, eventually, that became where I work most often. A lot of people who visit this area want to keep up with their practice while they're here and fitness is important to many locals, too. It's good for their bodies to balance out all that skiing and rock climbing."

"And running on the treadmill," he added, pointing a finger at his own chest.

"That, too," she agreed. "And I like to stay busy."

"You like to take care of people."

"Yes." She paused in the act of returning the mats to their place on the shelf. "The woman who currently owns the studio has offered to sell it to me."

"Perfect," he told her, taking the yoga mats from her hands. "When will that be finalized?"

She laughed. "Don't get ahead of yourself. I haven't agreed to anything."

"Why?"

"Owning a studio is a big responsibility."

"You've done it before, and you loved it."

"Things were different then."

"Things are different now."

She shook her head. "Not in the same way. I should get moving on breakfast." She started for the door. "Thanks for being game to do a session with me. I think—"

"Hold on." He placed his hands on her shoulders and spun her to face him. "Don't blow me off, April."

"I'm not."

"Why wouldn't you want to own a studio again?"

"Maybe I want to keep my options open. I have nothing tying me down right now. I can take off on a moment's notice if I want to. I'm a total free spirit."

At those words he flashed her a doubtful smile. "You're the least likely person to 'take off' that I know."

She bristled at the words, even though they were true.

"That's not a criticism. I like how grounded you are, but it's clear this community and the people in it mean something to you. This is your home. You love teaching yoga. Why wouldn't you want to have your own studio again? Is it the money? Because I—"

"It's not the money, and I'm not taking any of yours." She tried to pull away, but he held her steady. "What if I bought the studio and then I got sick again?" Unable to continue meeting his gaze, she focused on a small patch of sweat on the front of his T-shirt.

"What if you crossed the street and got hit by a car?" he asked in response.

"It's not the same thing."

"It is," he argued. "You've told me you've made it to the five-year-survival milestone. Even I know that's a big deal. Yes, there's a risk that you'll get sick again. There's a better chance that you'll stay healthy. There are no guarantees in life, and you can't just dump something that means so much to you because you're afraid it might not work."

"Does that apply only to me or are you going to take your own advice?"

"I finished the book."

"I'm not talking about the book," she snapped. "I'm

talking about the self-imposed isolation you plan to return to after Christmas. I'm talking about opening yourself to the possibility of being happy again. Of loving—"

"No." He released her so abruptly she stumbled back a step. "That part of me is gone. It died with Margo and Emmett."

"I've seen how you are with the girls," she argued. She wouldn't mention the way he made her feel. This wasn't about the two of them. This was him needing to admit he could love again. Even if it wasn't with her, he deserved a second chance at love. "You're not dead, Connor. You're here. Now."

"Don't try to fix me, April." The words weren't angry, only empty, which was worse. "I told you I don't have anything to give. I don't deserve..." He broke off, stalked to the edge of the room and back to her. "I'm not going there with you. If you want to live your simple little life, it's none of my business. In a few days, I'll be on a plane back to California. We have no hold on each other. Right now, what matters to both of us is Ranie and Shay. It's Christmas Eve, and I don't want to fight."

"Me neither," she whispered, although it was a lie. She wanted to push and prod this man until he admitted his heart was capable of mending. But he was right— she had no hold on him. And how could she pressure him for something she wasn't willing to give? Because in a few days, she'd be on a plane returning those girls to California. No matter what. "My friend Katie texted last night. She's closed the bakery to customers today and is hosting an open house for family and friends."

"I'm neither," he muttered.

"She invited all of us. I think it would be nice for the girls to get out of the cabin for a bit, and I'd like to pick up a few more Christmas gifts for them. I got some things when they first arrived, but tomorrow needs to be special."

"Everything you do is special," he whispered, and the honesty in his tone made her heart melt a little more.

No matter how frustrated he made her, she was a useless puddle of goo around this man. "Will you come with us?"

He shook his head. "I didn't handle a trip to town so well the last time."

"You're different now."

"It's been a week," he said with a wry smile.

She put aside her own worries and took his hand. "A lot can happen in a week."

He brushed a delicate kiss over her knuckles. "Why can't I say no to you?"

Chapter Ten

Why hadn't he said no?

Connor pressed two fingers to his forehead, which was throbbing so hard he thought a vein might actually pop. He stood off to the edge of the bakery, pretending to look at the display of mugs and small gifts housed on a farmhouse-style set of shelves. He could feel April's worried gaze and looked up long enough to give her a thumbs-up. She did the same and added a shoulder shrug and an apologetic smile.

But she had nothing to feel sorry about, and it was clear she belonged to this community and her friends. They'd been polite, if wary, when she'd made introductions earlier. He doubted there was a person in this room who didn't know his story, which made his skin prickle as if it were shrinking with every overly kind smile he received.

There seemed to be a line of people waiting to speak to her, and even now she was surrounded by a group of women who were taking turns giving her supportive hugs and gentle back pats. He wondered if they were sympathizing that she'd had to care for the broken-down author while the rest of them were enjoying Christmas vacation.

"That was the fakiest thumbs-up I've ever seen."

He turned to find Ranie at his side, arms crossed over her chest in her signature posture.

"*Fakiest* isn't a word."

"Neither is fun if this party is any indication."

He nodded at where Shay was busy at a café table, decorating cookies with a group of children her age. "Your sister might disagree."

"Because she's a little kid."

He arched a brow. "And you're so wise and mature?"

A dismissive sniff was his answer.

"I can ask around to see if there are any Christmas pageants being performed tonight. We might find you a gig as one of the three wise guys who visited the baby Jesus."

"You're not like other adults," she answered after a moment.

He nodded. "I'm real messed up."

"I'd say you're just real. Everyone else looks at me like they know exactly what happened with my mom. April's friends are nice, but they give me extralong hugs and I don't even know them."

"Hugs aren't too bad."

"You don't give out a lot of hugs," she countered.

He made his voice even. "Do you want one?"

"No. I just don't want people to pretend like nothing's wrong when they look at me as if I'm some baby bird with a broken wing. Like they have to be extra careful."

"I like that imagery," he told her. "Have you ever thought about writing down your thoughts?"

"Like in a diary?" she asked.

"Sure. A journal works. Or poems. Or whatever interests you."

"Did you keep a journal after your wife and son died?"

"I kept a tight grip on the liquor bottle."

She barked out a laugh. "I don't think you're supposed to admit that to a kid."

"You like real, remember." He put a hand on her back, not quite a hug, but letting her know she wasn't alone. "Losing a family member changes you. It's a hole that can't be filled." He believed the words, but lately the hole inside him hadn't felt so cavernous.

"I think it takes time," Ranie told him. "At least that's what the adults say."

"They say that because they're afraid of your sadness, and hope is an easy thing to offer."

Her blue eyes flicked to him, and he cursed himself. What the hell was wrong with his mood? He wasn't supposed to be bringing down a twelve-year-old girl with his own baggage. That was a total jerk move.

"I'm sorry," he said quickly. "Don't pay any attention to me."

"April's pretty good at filling holes," she said softly.

"Yep." He looked to where April stood, the circle of friends surrounding her bigger than it was a few minutes earlier. She touched the woman in front of her on the cheek and then wrapped her in a tight hug. His heart sped up. "She gives good hugs, too."

Ranie groaned. "Eww. Don't corrupt me."

At that moment, a tall, strapping man with blond hair, blue eyes and shoulders wide enough to look at home on a football field approached them. A boy who looked to be a year or two older than Ranie was with him.

"I'm Logan Travers," he said, holding out a hand. "Josh's brother."

Connor shook his hand. "Connor Pierce."

"You're the one staying at Cloud Cabin?"

"I am."

"I built that cabin."

"You do good work."

Logan nudged forward the boy next to him. "This is Jordan Dempsey. He lives here in town." The boy said a quiet "hello, sir" and grasped Connor's hand.

"Nice to meet you, Jordan." Connor turned to his side before realizing Ranie had stepped all the way behind him. He moved so she could be seen, earning him a dark look. "This is Ranie. She's staying with April over the holidays."

"Hey," she whispered, offering a small wave to Logan and Jordan.

Logan nudged Jordan again. The boy cleared his throat. "It sucks about your mom. My dad left town a while back so I don't see him, but at least I know he's still alive."

Ranie stared at the kid for a minute then said, "Um…thanks…I think."

Logan placed a large hand on Jordan's back. "Too

much information, buddy. Didn't you want to ask her something?"

"Oh, right. Katie has a basketball net out back. Do you want to go shoot some hoops? Otherwise, they're going to rope us into helping the little kids with their cookies."

As if on cue, Katie glanced from the crowded cookie table in their direction.

Connor cleared his throat. "Ranie likes—"

"Sure," she said, stepping fully away from Connor. He had the ridiculous urge to pull her back. She glanced up at him. "Will you let April know where I went?"

He nodded. "Don't go anywhere else, and come right back in if you need me."

She gave him a funny look. "Need you for what?"

From somewhere long forgotten, he summoned his best fatherly stare. "Anything."

"Relax," she whispered. "It's just basketball." She turned to Jordan. "You lead the way, but I have to warn you I'm not very good."

"Doesn't matter," he said. "Anything is better than putting sprinkles on cookies."

Connor watched as they disappeared through the swinging metal door behind the display counter.

"He's a good boy," Logan said.

Connor felt his eyes narrow. "He better be." Unfamiliar protective instincts raged through him. "She's young."

"They're both kids. Are you close to April and the two girls?"

Connor blinked as his mind registered how his attitude must look. "Not exactly. But I'm looking out for them while I'm here."

"Josh told me you're a writer."

"Uh-huh."

"Pretty famous, right?"

"In some circles."

Logan let out a deep laugh. "For someone who makes a living with words, you sure don't use many of them when you speak."

"What do you want to talk about?" Connor asked with a sidelong glance. "My dead wife and kid?"

To his credit, Logan didn't react to the rude and inappropriate question. "About as much as I want to unload about the drunk-driving accident that killed my sister."

Connor closed his eyes and let out a breath. The thing about being so wrapped up in his own grief was that he forgot that his story, while tragic, wasn't new or even all that rare. Most people carried pain or tragedy within them. It was only a matter of who could cope the best. He hated to admit that he'd felt a lot like Ranie at this gathering, mistrustful of the kindness in the eyes of the people he met and sure that all they felt for him was pity.

He'd been too long out of the real world. He'd had friends in California once, but he'd cut them out of his life after the accident. In doing so, he'd forgotten how to act like a normal person. April was helping him, giving him strength with her unconditional caring. He owed it to her to make an effort.

He laughed since that was exactly what he'd promised her.

"Something funny about my sister's death?" Logan asked, his tone icy as the top of a fourteener in a blizzard.

"No, of course not." Connor turned fully to face the other man. "I'm sorry. I was laughing at my own ignorance and insensitivity, although come to think of it, neither of those is funny." He shrugged. "Basically, I'm a jackass."

Logan stared at him for a moment, then threw back his head and laughed. "When you decide to use the words, you sure do make them count."

Make an effort. Make his words count.

If Connor took only those two maxims from his time in Colorado, it would be a gift he could never hope to repay. He might not be able to make the changes April wanted him to, but he could begin the promise of rebuilding a life outside the walls of his apartment.

"Tell me more about building Cloud Cabin," he said to Logan, and started down the path of once again becoming part of the world around him.

"Wake up, April. It's Christmas. Santa found us."

April blinked several times as her eyes adjusted to the faint light of her bedroom. Only a dim cast of blue light filtered in through the curtains, which meant the sun hadn't yet risen. There was a weight on top of her that she quickly realized was Shay. The girl's face was only inches from hers.

A sticky finger tapped on her cheeks. "Are you awake yet?"

"I'm awake," she said around a yawn. "What time is it?"

"Time for Christmas presents," Shay shouted, hopping off the bed to flip on the light switch.

April shaded her eyes with one hand as she struggled to wake up. Normally, she was an early bird, but she wasn't sure this hour even counted as morning. Add in the fact that Connor had kept her awake until the wee hours of the night, and she was definitely not at her perkiest.

"It's too early for this," Ranie muttered from the doorway. Apparently, April wasn't the only one who could have used more sleep.

She swung her legs over the side of the bed and pointed at Shay. "Are you eating a candy cane?"

The girl flashed a wide smile. "Santa filled our stockings, too. Connor said I could pick one thing."

"Breakfast of champions," Connor said, appearing in the doorway behind Ranie.

"You're awake already?"

"And I made coffee." He stepped into the room and handed her a steaming mug.

"Oh, thank you," she said with a grateful breath. "I lo—" She ducked her head. "You're the best."

"Can we open presents now?" Shay was practically buzzing with energy. It had been a long time since April had witnessed a child's excitement on Christmas morning. As tired as she was, she couldn't help but smile.

"Give me a minute to wash my face and I'll be down," April told her.

"Your face isn't even dirty," Shay complained.

"Let's go, squirt." Connor took Shay's shoulders and turned her toward the door. "You can count your presents while you wait."

Her eyes wide, Shay darted from the room and Ranie followed.

Connor turned and cupped April's face in his hands. "Merry Christmas," he whispered with a gentle kiss. He tasted of toothpaste and spice, and April realized that the taste of him was just one more thing she'd miss when he was gone.

She forced a smile, determined not to let thoughts of losing him crowd her mind today. "You know, I didn't fill stockings last night," she told him. After the girls had gone to bed, she and Connor had wrapped the gifts she'd bought and placed them under the tree.

"Maybe Santa Claus really paid a visit to the cabin," he said with a wink.

She kissed him again and he took the mug from her hands, placing it on top of the dresser so he could pull her in tight. After a few minutes, she moved away, her breath ragged. "I need to get moving. Counting presents will only keep her busy for so long."

"I can buy you some time." He pressed one more kiss to the tip of her nose. "I'll have her put on boots so we can go outside and look for reindeer prints."

She stopped at the door to the bathroom, glanced over her shoulder. "Hoofprints?"

He ran a hand through his hair, looking almost embarrassed. "You know they leave a trail of sparkles on the ground under where they take off."

"I actually did *not* know that. Connor Pierce, you've been hiding your holiday spirit."

"Merry Christmas," he said with a smile, and then he was gone.

Just as April walked down the stairs fifteen minutes later, Connor and the girls were stomping back into the house, their boots coated with fresh snow.

"I saw the reindeer tracks," Shay called, slipping off

her coat and boots and rushing toward April. "They left red and silver sparkles in the snow."

Even Ranie looked impressed. "It was cool," she said, and glanced at Connor before picking up the coat Shay had dropped on the floor and hanging it on a peg.

April took Connor's cold hand as he came toward her, and laced her fingers with his. "How did you know to make reindeer prints?" she whispered.

"It was one of Emmett's favorite things about Christmas morning."

April smiled around the lump in her throat. "Thank you for sharing that tradition with us."

"Come on, people," Shay called impatiently from the family room. "We're ready to open presents now."

April settled on the couch with Connor across from her in one of the leather club chairs. "Let the Christmas madness begin," he announced.

Shay let out a squeal of delight, but instead of digging into her own gifts, she took two small bags from deep under the tree and handed one to April and the other to Connor. "Open them," she said, her cheeks flushed and her eyes bright. "They're from Ranie and me."

April swiped her fingers under her eyes and sniffed. "Are you sure you don't want to start with your gifts?"

Shay shook her head.

"They're not a big deal," Ranie said, her eyes watchful.

April started to assure her they were, but Connor said, "Let's open them and find out."

The girl grinned at him, and April was once again amazed at the bond that had formed so quickly between the three of them. All of their rough edges seemed to fit together perfectly, and another wave of sadness washed over her knowing Ranie might not get that type of understanding from her uncle in California. The kind of soul-deep knowing she'd be lucky to have from any other man in her life.

"Are you gonna cry the happy tears again?" Shay asked.

"Probably," April admitted, and tore off the wrapping paper on the small package. Inside was a pinecone figure. The arms and legs were pipe cleaners, and plastic googly eyes had been glued to what would be the head. Wrapped in one pipe-cleaner arm was a small roll of blue felt.

"We made them while you were sick with the craft kits you bought us." Shay placed a finger on the felt. "This is your yoga mat. Connor has a book."

"I love it," April whispered, and glanced at Connor. He was staring at the pinecone figure, a slight smile tugging one corner of his mouth. "Let me see yours, Connor."

He held it up, and she noticed his hand was shaking just a little. "The book says '#1 bestseller' on the cover."

"That's what you want, right?" Ranie asked.

"Yes," he said softly. "Thank you both. This is a *very* big deal."

April pulled Shay in for a tight hug. "Thank you so much. I'll keep it forever."

"Put them on the coffee table," Shay said, her eyes dancing. "We made ones for Ranie and me, too. They can all be together."

The waiting Christmas gifts momentarily forgotten, Shay ran to a corner of the room, bent at one of the low cabinets under the bookshelf and pulled out two smaller decorated pinecones. She ran back over and arranged the Connor-and-April pinecones on either side of the smaller two.

"It's a pinecone family," she said, and April's heart cracked in two. They weren't a family. These two weeks were like make-believe, a time Shay would remember years from now as a fuzzy series of events, if she thought of this holiday at all. Or maybe the memory these girls would hold hadn't even been made yet. What if what they carried with them was the impending end? The point where the woman their mother had entrusted with their future walked away because she was too scared to commit to them.

"They look great," April managed, her throat raw from the effort of holding back tears.

"They were Shay's idea," Ranie said, looking between April and Connor as if she couldn't figure out what about a few decorated pinecones was making the adults react so strangely.

Connor cleared his throat. "How about I put them on the mantel to be safe and you girls start on your gifts?"

"Presents!" Shay shouted, oblivious to the effect her sweet gifts had.

She dropped to her knees next to the tree, and April pulled out her phone. "Let me get a few pictures of you."

Shay posed for a couple of seconds, then reached for a brightly wrapped package. "I can't wait any longer."

Connor came to sit next to April as Shay held up a bright pink princess costume. "Oh, it's just what I wanted," she said, and twirled in a happy circle. "You next, Ranie."

The girl held a wrapped box on her lap. "Is everyone going to watch?"

"Yes," Shay said with an exasperated sigh. "You know we each take turns opening presents."

Ranie sniffed. "Maybe April does it different."

"That sounds perfect to me," April told her, and got an eye roll in return.

"We don't have all morning here, kid." Connor rubbed his stomach. "Breakfast casserole is waiting."

Again, April was about to scold him for his attitude, but Ranie smiled. "Give me a break. It's not even seven a.m."

"You get the point," Connor shot back. "No more delays. I command you to open that gift."

"As if you're the boss of me," Ranie said, and stuck out her tongue. But she was already carefully unfolding the corners of the wrapping paper.

"Why does she like you so much," April whispered while Ranie was distracted with her gift, "when you're so mean?"

Connor scoffed. "I'm not mean. I'm direct. There's a difference." He linked their hands together. "Sometimes she takes things too seriously, especially herself. It breaks her out of it when I give her a little grief."

"Unorthodox therapy," April said, "but no denying it works."

Ranie gasped as she pulled a pair of designer sheepskin boots out of the box. Her eyes flicked to April. "These are the boots I saw when we got to Colorado that first day," she said, her voice soft. "You said they were too much money with everything else."

April smiled. "Christmas is about going a little overboard. Do you like them?"

"I love them." Ranie stood and came to April, giving her a small hug. "Thank you so much. They're perfect."

"Wow. You're welcome. I'm glad you like them."

Shay grabbed another gift. "Me next."

The girls continued to open presents until there was nothing left under the tree. Ranie was more animated than April had ever seen, and it tugged on her heart in a way she didn't want to examine. She knew Jill had been sick for a while and wondered exactly how much responsibility Ranie had taken on in the house and if she'd ever been able to be a carefree kid.

"How about stockings?" Connor asked.

Shay jumped up and ran toward the fireplace. "I love stockings!"

Connor handed the girls theirs and then placed one decorated with a needlepoint angel stitched on the front in April's lap.

"You didn't have to get me anything," she told him.

"I know. That's what makes it Christmas."

Ranie's harsh gasp drew April's attention. "Are these real?" the girl asked, her eyes wide on Connor.

He nodded. "You have pierced ears, right?"

"Yes, but..." She held up a pair of tiny diamond earrings. "I've never had anything like this."

"Merry Christmas," he said, almost sheepishly.

"Oh, it's so pretty." A delicate gold bracelet dangled from Shay's fingers.

"What's the charm on it?" April asked, leaning closer.

"It's the sun."

"Perfect for you, Shay, because you are a ray of sunshine."

The young girl beamed. "Now you, April."

April pulled out a small box from her stocking. "Do I sense a theme?"

Connor shrugged. "I snuck out of the party to shop but didn't want to be gone too long. There's a jewelry store next to the bakery."

"You really didn't have to—"

"Open the gift, April."

Unwrapping the shiny paper, April felt like a kid. Other than an annual Secret Santa exchange at the yoga studio and the occasional White Elephant party, she hadn't received a Christmas gift in years. As she opened the velvet box inside, her breath caught in her throat.

She glanced up at Connor, whose expression was an adorable mix of hope and nerves. "I'm out of practice with gift giving," he said softly, "but diamonds are always good, right?"

"These are better than good." She fingered the delicate diamond hoops. "They're perfect." The earrings were understated and gorgeous, and she could wear them every day, even to a yoga class. The last man who had bought her jewelry had been her ex-husband.

He'd insisted on her wearing large and sometimes gaudy stones, as if having a wife decked out in jewels helped prove his status within the Hollywood community. The jewelry had been the first thing she'd sold to pay off her medical bills.

"Try them on," Shay said, and with trembling hands, April fastened an earring in each ear.

"They look nice," Ranie told her.

At that moment Jingle came bounding into the room and pounced on a stray bow. The girls laughed, both jumping up to play with the kitten.

"Thank you," April told Connor as he tucked her hair behind one ear. She leaned forward and brushed a soft kiss across his lips.

"There's something else in the stocking," he said.

"Connor, no," She shook her head. "I thought we were just doing gifts for the girls. I don't have anything—"

"You've given me so much already." He cupped her face with a tenderness that brought another round of tears to her eyes. "Let me do this."

She dug in the bottom of the stocking and pulled out… "A flash drive?" She gave him a crooked smile. "Thanks. I can always use—"

"My new book is on it. I know it's already with the editor, but I was hoping you'd read it, too. I mean if you have time and—"

She threw her arms around him, burying her face in his neck so he wouldn't see how much she was affected by his gesture. For Connor to share something so personal with her, it must mean…no. She wouldn't let herself go there. She couldn't allow the hope for more to creep into her mind and her heart. It would only make the end harder to bear. "This is turning out to be an amazing Christmas" she whispered instead.

"Yes, it is," he agreed, and held her close.

Chapter Eleven

Connor ended the call with his editor and walked back into the cabin's bright kitchen. "Who wants to play a game of cards?"

"I do," Shay answered, bouncing on her knees on the chair. "So does Jingle."

Connor scooped up the kitten, which was pawing at the downturned cards Connor had left on the table. "Are you feeding this thing rocks?" He set the kitten onto the floor and watched him dart to the other side of the room. "He's probably doubled his weight since we found him."

April lightly pounded her palm on the table. "Hey, let's focus here. What did your editor think of the book? She loved it, right? Of course she loved it, because it's a fantastic story. It's flawless. Un-put-downable."

"That's not a word," Ranie said, but she was smiling.

"It should be," April countered. "I have bags under my eyes from staying up half the night to finish it."

Connor didn't bother to point out that reading wasn't the only reason she'd been up late, and he tried to ignore the fact that April's praise for his story meant more than anything his editor had said to him.

"What did she say?" April asked again.

"She liked it."

She raised her brows. "Liked?"

"Maybe she used the words 'guaranteed bestseller.'" Connor ducked his head, feeling color rise to his cheeks. That wasn't possible. He was a guy. Guys didn't blush. But he'd never felt comfortable with hearing praise for his work. Writing was personal for him, the characters milling about his head as the story formed and took a life of its own. He molded and shaped them, but they still came from a very private part of who he was. It was the piece he'd thought he'd lost when Margo and Emmett died. The part that April had helped him rediscover.

She and the girls gave a great cheer. He saw April start to rise from her chair, then lower back down again, folding her hands together on the table so tightly her knuckles turned white.

"Congratulations," she said, and the tone of her voice had changed to a hollow, thready rasp. "It looks like our work here is done."

He sucked in a breath as both girls turned to stare at her. He knew what she meant. His flight back to California was scheduled in two days. In the excitement of Christmas and keeping the girls busy, they'd been avoiding the inevitable conversation about him leaving. He still wasn't ready to tackle it.

But now that April had broached the subject, Ranie took up the mantle.

"Did you talk to Aunt Tracy?" she asked, glancing at Jingle, who was chasing the shadow cast on the floor in front of the window by the branches bobbing in the winter wind.

April bit down on her lip. "I did, and apparently your cousin Tommy is allergic to cats."

Ranie shook her head. "That's not true. They used to have a cat. I remember it."

"Obviously, something has changed," April snapped, and then ducked her head as if she regretted it. "I'm sorry, but you knew there was a good chance you wouldn't be able to bring Jingle to California. It's why I didn't want—"

"I don't want to go to California." Shay threw her cards on the table and jumped from her chair. "The twins are gross. They burp and fart and Tommy eats his boogers." She bent and lifted Jingle into her arms.

April's heart stuttered as the kitten nuzzled into the little girl's neck. "They're boys, sweetie, but they'll get better." She glanced at Connor for support.

"Just watch out if they try to 'Dutch oven' you," he said, pointing at each girl.

Ranie grimaced. "I don't even want to know what that is."

"It's when—"

April slashed the air with her hand. "Not helping, Connor."

"Why can't we stay here with you?" Shay asked.

The question, which had been running on a constant loop inside April's head for the past few days, still shocked her. Hearing the words spoken in Shay's sweet voice was like a punch to her heart.

"I would love to keep you," April told her, making her voice soft, "but Aunt Tracy is your family. She understands—"

"We don't even know her," Shay argued. "She won't let us keep Jingle and there are so many dumb rules in her house."

"She's a good mom to her boys." April could feel desperation rising like a tidal wave up her spine. She needed to convince these girls she was doing the right thing. But how was she supposed to when she couldn't quite believe it herself? "She'll take care of you."

"We want you to take care of us." The kitten mewed as Shay squeezed him tighter.

April's gaze flicked to Ranie, but the girl was staring at the floor, her arms held tight to her side. "I can't," she whispered.

"We'll be good," Shay said, and the fact that she thought April's refusal had anything to do with who she and her sister were or how they acted was another painful stab inside April. "We won't eat much, and we can help—"

"I might die," April yelled suddenly, and the silence that followed was so charged she expected to see electricity sparking the air around them.

Shay let out a small whimper.

"I'm sorry." April took a step closer to the girl, but Shay backed up until her legs hit the couch. "After everything you went through with your mommy, I can't bear the thought of putting you girls at risk of watching me get sick again."

Ranie moved until she was standing next to her sister. "You're not sick," she muttered between clenched teeth. "You just don't want us."

"That's not—"

The cat meowed and squirmed in Shay's arms, jumping to the floor and darting from the room. Shay started to follow, tears streaming down her face, then stopped and turned to April. "We don't want you right back," she screamed. "I hate you."

April sucked in a shattered breath and watched the young girl disappear up the stairs. She turned to Ranie. "I'm sorry. I don't want her to be upset. I'll make her understand."

The girl only glared at her. "She already does," she said, and followed her sister.

April watched her go, wanting to reach out but knowing she had nothing to offer either of the girls. She rounded on Connor. "You could have helped me," she snapped. "You could have helped me make it better for them. I can't keep them. They need to understand I'm too big a risk."

His green eyes, which this morning had been so full of light and affection, were blank as he stared at her. "Life is a risk," he said. "What you're giving those girls is a lame excuse."

"Lame?" she sputtered. "I had breast cancer, Connor. The same disease that killed their mother. I could get sick again. That's real. I could die."

He gave a laugh so odd and disturbing it made the hair on the back of her neck stand on end. "You could die tomorrow," he whispered. "You could step off a curb and get hit by a car. That's real, April. Life is a risk, and sending those girls away isn't doing them any favors. It isn't helping them. It's being a coward."

The truth of his words sliced through her, and all her pent-up fear and pain poured forth, flooding her with everything she'd tried to repress for so long. All the ways she was lacking stood out in stark relief, and she hated it. Hated herself at this moment. Hated Connor Pierce.

"Don't talk to me about being a coward," she said, her breath coming out in shallow pants. "Not when you're packing to return to your cutoff life, alone and hiding out and using your grief as a weapon against anyone who tries to get close to you."

"That's not what I do," he ground out.

"Then don't leave," she told him, and gasped at her own boldness. She hadn't meant to say the words, but she was too raw and open now to hold them back any longer. "Stay here with me, Connor. Help me be brave. Give me your strength and I'll give you mine and together we can—"

"There is no 'we.'" His voice was so cold it sent a chill through her.

"I love you," she said without thinking.

He shook his head. "Don't say that."

"You know it's true whether I speak the words or not." She took a step toward him, another piece of her heart shattering when he flinched away from her touch. "I know you feel—"

"You know nothing about me." His jaw was clenched so tightly his mouth barely moved as he spit the words at her.

"I know you want to pretend you don't care, but it's a lie." She pointed to the stairs. "You care about those girls. You care about me. You are still alive, Connor." She jabbed a finger at his chest. "In here."

He grabbed her hand and yanked it away from his body. "I see what you're doing, April. Everyone sees it. You make your whole life about other people, what they care about and what they need. You think if you work hard enough for your friends, they'll mistake that for you truly being involved. But you're just as cutoff as I am. We're the same, and we both know how this is going to end. How it was always meant to end. It ends with both of us alone. What if I said yes to you? What if I told you right now that I want to make a life with you and the girls? We could be a family if you just said the word. How would you answer?"

She swallowed, her gut suddenly twisted. *This is what you wanted,* she told herself. But she couldn't force her mouth to form the word *yes.* She wanted to. Wanted to mend the hearts of those girls upstairs. And she certainly didn't want to admit that she'd let fear rule her life. Yet, how could she deny it?

She bit down on her lip for several moments before finally asking, "What does it matter how I'd answer? You're not asking the question, are you?"

"Not when you're too afraid to answer it," he whispered, and walked past her.

April glanced around the kitchen and sucked in a harsh breath. There was a stack of Shay's drawings on the counter and the cards from the abandoned game were still strewn across the table. It was so different from her neat and tidy apartment.

Two weeks on the mountain and this cabin felt like home. The girls and Connor were the family she secretly craved. But he was right. She was scared to claim that future. If she got sick again, what would happen if they left her? What if she wasn't perfect, couldn't take care of them and everyone walked away? What if watching them leave broke her heart in a way she couldn't mend?

Connor heard footsteps pounding down the stairs as he stared at his computer several hours later. The bluish glow of the screen was bright in the fading light of afternoon, casting shadows across the wool rug and hardwood floor. His editor had emailed again, this time to say they were fast-tracking the publication of his book and asking about dates for a possible six-city book tour.

The thought of traveling the country and standing in front of groups of readers made his stomach jump and turn. He'd managed the holiday party in Crimson because of April and the girls. To face people, to pretend to be human on his own, was a daunting prospect. But April had been right in what she'd accused him of in the kitchen. He was a coward, afraid to put himself out there again, and risk hurt and heartbreak.

Margo would expect more. His beautiful wife would have wanted him to be happy. She would have expected him to start to live again.

April shouted his name, her tone so chilling it made goose bumps rise on his skin. He raced to the edge of the hallway.

"It's Shay," she called from the bottom of the stairs, already shoving her feet into snow boots. "She's gone."

"And so is Jingle," Ranie said on a sob. "She took him and—"

"No." Connor hadn't realized he'd shouted the word until both of them glanced up. "I mean, that's impossible. It's freezing out, and it only stopped snow-ing a few hours ago. She must be hiding, playing a trick because she's angry."

Ranie shook her head. The girl was panting for breath, her blue eyes wide and terrified against skin pale as a December moon. "I've looked everywhere, and she wouldn't do that anyway. Shay is afraid to be alone."

He thundered down the steps and grabbed his coat. "Then why would she run away?"

"I don't know," Ranie said on a sob. "She was so upset about Jingle. They're gone."

"We'll find both of them," April told her.

"This is your fault," Ranie screamed. "She ran away because you won't let us stay."

Connor saw April's head jerk back as if the girl had struck her.

"There's no time for that now," he said, laying a hand on Ranie's shoulder. "We all need to look for your sister."

He opened the back door and held up a hand. "I can see her boot prints," he said, pointing to the tracks in the snow leading toward the woods. "And it looks like...damn it."

"What?" April tried to peer around his shoulder. He took a step out into the fading sunlight and crouched low. "Look at the tiny paw prints mixed up with hers. It looks like Jingle got out and she went after him."

"Oh, no." April's gaze followed his. "They disappear into the forest."

"We need to find her soon," Connor said, looking at the girl's small tracks. The sun hung low over the craggy peak that rose to the west of the cabin. "Before we lose the light. We only have about an hour."

He shouted for Shay at the top of his lungs. The only answer was a hollow echo and the sound of a squirrel scurrying along a branch.

"She hasn't been out here long," April said, and her voice sounded like a plea. She called for Shay as well, but received no response. "Should I call the sheriff?"

Connor shook his head. "They'll take too long to get up here. Damn it," he repeated. "There are two sets of tracks. It's like the kitten was running back and forth at the edge of the forest and Shay was following. I can't tell which way she went."

Ranie let out a pained whimper. "We need to find her." She rubbed her gloved hands together. "It's freezing out here and her coat was still hanging by the door."

"We will," Connor said, letting no trace of doubt slip into his tone. "We're going to split up. You two take the south and west side of the house. I'll cover the north and east and check around the caretaker's cabin. Call for her and keep looking for tracks. She's out here."

April nodded but her eyes were as panicked as the girl's. Connor grabbed her arms and gave her a little shake. "We're going to find her. I need you to believe me."

"I do," she said without hesitation. She swallowed and then gave a more forceful nod. "I believe you." She gently nudged Ranie and they both headed to the far side of the cabin, taking turns yelling for Shay.

As their voices became fainter, Connor started calling again. He stood in place for a moment, studying the puzzle of footprints, trying to determine which way the girl had gone.

Icy tendrils of panic buzzed up his spine and before he'd taken one step, he was transported back to the accident. It was like reliving a nightmare, images flashing in his mind as his body heaved under the weight of his failure.

Suddenly he was no longer on a snow-covered mountain. It was a rainy night on a curvy California highway and he could feel the heat of the flames licking at him as he tried to run, tried to find the strength to move toward the burning car. The mental picture changed again and he was on his knees, the car exploding in front of him. The heat from the fire burned his eyes and he blinked, suddenly finding himself on all fours in the snow, white and icy under his hands, the chilled wetness seeping in through his pant legs.

Not again.

The two words were like a mantra as he forced himself to stand. This was not that horrible night. He would not fail Shay the way he had his wife and son. He was strong now, capable. He wouldn't allow his fear and his weakness to paralyze him the way they had after the accident.

He examined the footprints again and then headed into the woods, his boots crunching in the snow. After taking a few more steps, he glanced over his shoulder and realized that due to the hill behind the cabin, he could no longer see either of the structures. Everything around him was a mix of white, brown and green, and it was clear how a young girl could have gotten quickly turned around.

Daylight was quickly fading, sending shadows across the ground and making it more difficult to see her trail. He continued to call and if he had to admit it, began to pray. Not to God or some higher spirit—his faith was too shattered for that. Instead, he allowed his heart to reach out to Margo, wherever she might be.

"Help me," he whispered into the silence of the forest. "Help me rescue that little girl the way I should have saved you and Emmett."

His chest squeezed as he reached out to the woman he'd lost, or maybe to nothing. He was desperate enough at this moment not to care. An icy wind blew through the trees, battering his exposed skin, and he shouted Shay's name again.

This time when he listened for a response, there was…something. A soft whine from somewhere in the trees. His gaze darted around until it fell on a flash of color and he moved toward it as fast as he could in the snow, pushing branches out of the way as he went. He rounded a rock formation and saw a pair of pink snow boots sticking out from under the branches of an enormous pine tree.

"Shay," he shouted again, dropping to his knees and scooping her into his arms.

She blinked several times, relief clear in her sweet blue eyes, and then bent her head. "Jingle ran away," she whispered, her voice hoarse. "But I found him. I'm keeping him safe."

"I know, sweetheart," he whispered, seeing the kitten's black head poke out from her fuzzy sweatshirt. Her skin was pale, her tiny rosebud lips tinged with blue. He unzipped his coat and shrugged out of it as best he could without letting go of Shay. Wrapping her and the kitten in the thick down, he held her close and walked as quickly as he could back to the cabin.

"Stay awake, Shay," he told her. "April and your sister want to see your beautiful smile when we get back."

She gave a tiny nod, but her eyes drifted closed.

Connor yelled for April as he made his way through the trees and snow-covered debris of the forest floor. Every time he shouted, Shay opened her eyes, which he hoped was a good sign. She was shivering like an aspen leaf in a strong wind. He tripped over a fallen log and she jerked, the kitten mewling pathetically as he righted himself.

He heard April's answering call, and Ranie ran to the edge of the property to meet him as he came into the clearing. "Is she okay?"

"She'll be fine," he answered, hoping with everything he was that he told the girl the truth. April was at his side a moment later.

"Oh, Shay," she murmured, her worried gaze clashing with his.

"We need to get her inside," he said, forcing himself to remain calm and focus on the action it would take to warm the half-frozen child.

April nodded and when she turned her head, he realized she was on her cell phone. "I've got Jake Travers on the line. He wants to know if she's responsive?"

"Yes, she spoke to me. She seemed tired but lucid."

She repeated his words into the phone. "She's pale but her breathing seems regular. It'll be hard to tell until we get her into the house."

Ranie was crying quietly on his other side. "We're going to take care of her," he assured her, again with a confidence he wasn't sure he felt.

April disconnected and ran ahead, holding the cabin's door open for them. "Jake says to change her out of anything wet and use dry heat to warm her, starting at the center of her body. He's on his way up to check on her."

He stomped the snow off his boots as he entered the cabin, then headed up the stairs to her room. "Shay, honey, are you awake?"

"I'll get a heating pad," April said from behind him.

The girl shifted in his arms, one side of her mouth curving into a faint smile. "Jingle's tickling me," she murmured, and then breathed out a sigh. He lifted the kitten away from her and handed him to Ranie, who wrapped her hands around the animal and held it close.

From what Connor could see, Jingle hadn't suffered any ill effects of his time exposed to the cold, likely because Shay had kept him warm with the heat from her body. He wondered if the cat had any idea how lucky he was to be loved by that little girl.

"Shay, you're going to be okay," Ranie said as Connor removed Shay's boots and his coat, then pulled back the covers and lowered her to the sheets. "Do you hear me?"

Shay's eyes fluttered open and she looked directly at her sister. "I saw Mommy," she whispered. "She was so pretty, Ranie, like she was before." Another wispy smile flitted across her face as her eyes closed again.

A flash of envy stabbed through Connor at the idea of seeing his wife and son again in the way he imagined Shay was describing. Almost immediately, he put the thought aside, because he didn't want to think what it might mean if Shay was having visions of her dead mother.

Ranie started to cry harder and, moving on instincts rusty from years of not being used, Connor wrapped his arms around the girl and murmured words of encouragement against her hair. No jokes, no teasing. Just the support of an adult for a child in need.

After a few moments, he turned her to face him and bent to look in her eyes. "She's going to be okay. I promise." He wasn't sure what prompted him to say those words, since he no basis on which to make that pledge. He offered up a silent plea to Margo for help, then took a deep breath.

"We're not helping her this way," he told Ranie firmly. "We need to believe she's going to be okay."

April hurried into the room. "Jake texted. He just turned onto the mountain road." She held a heating pad in her hand. "Let's do our best to warm her until he gets here."

Connor dropped a soft kiss on the top of Ranie's head. "I promise," he repeated, and started the process of warming the younger girl.

Chapter Twelve

April stood in the doorway to the girls' bedroom late that night, the hallway light illuminating the darkness enough that she could see the two of them curled up together under the covers of Shay's twin bed. Jingle was wedged between them, purring contentedly.

Jake had given the girl a thorough examination, and Shay had woken long enough to eat a bit of soup. April was so thankful that Shay seemed to be on her way to a full recovery.

According to what the girl told them, she'd opened the cabin's door to check the temperature before going out to play and Jingle had darted onto the porch and across the driveway. Without watching where she was going, she'd chased him into the woods, but by the time he'd finally slowed enough that she could catch him, she hadn't been able to find her way back to the cabin.

The thought of Shay lost in the frozen woods with darkness approaching still sent panic spiraling through April's gut. She couldn't imagine what would have happened if Connor hadn't found the girl when he did.

There was no talk about how angry Shay and Ranie had been with her earlier. April's belief that Shay had run away to punish her now seemed petty. The one good thing about her terror was that it put everything else into perspective. As Connor had said, life could change in an instant and she wasn't going to waste another minute living in fear.

She felt Connor's presence behind her and shifted so that he could stand next to her.

"It's a miracle that Shay's okay," she whispered.

His breath hitched but he nodded.

She leaned into his arm. "You saved her."

"You and Ranie would have found her if you'd been in the right area of the forest."

Shay hummed softly in her sleep and scooted toward Ranie, who automatically pulled her closer.

April quietly closed the door and laced her fingers with Connor's, leading him down the hall to her bedroom.

"I shouldn't…" he said, but didn't pull away. "My flight goes out early tomorrow and—"

"I need to talk to you," she interrupted. "Please."

His jaw tightened, but he nodded.

Nerves and fear and hope wove together in April's chest, making her heart beat like she'd just summited one of the high peaks that surrounded Crimson. "You were right." She bit down on her lip to keep from shouting the words at the top of her lungs. "You were right," she repeated in a quieter tone.

His brows furrowed. "About what?"

"About me living in fear. I've been letting the past dominate my life, which has kept me from the future I want. But I'm through with that. I'm going to keep the girls, Connor."

He sucked in a breath.

"At least," she clarified, "I'm going to ask them if they still want to stay with me. I hurt them by not committing sooner, and I have a lot of mistakes to rectify. But Jill entrusted them to me, and I want to honor her wishes."

"Because you feel obligated?" he asked carefully.

"Because I love them," she answered with a smile. "Having them with me is a gift, and I'm not going to throw it away. The future isn't a guarantee, but I'm meant to be their family, and they're supposed to be mine." She squeezed his hands. "Just like I hope you'll be mine."

His fingers slipped from hers. "I don't understand. This morning you were so sure."

"This morning I was stupid and afraid." She laughed. "I'm still afraid, but who isn't? I won't let it rule my life. Ask me again, Connor. The question from this morning about making a family with you and the girls."

She could see his chest rise and fall and she wanted to reach for him, to see if his heart was beating a crazy rhythm that matched her own.

"I didn't actually ask anything." He ran a hand through his hair. "I only proposed the possibility of a question."

The word *proposed* had a lovely ring to it coming from this man. "Such a stickler for language," she chided gently. "You know what I mean. Ask me now." She let everything she felt show in her eyes and held her bruised heart out to him.

His face went completely blank.

Not a good sign.

"I..." He turned, placed his palms against the top of the dresser as if he needed the support. "I told you my heart died with Margo and Emmett."

She shook her head. "I don't believe you."

"It doesn't matter."

"That's not true." She laid her hand on his arm, the lightest touch, in an attempt to gentle him. April understood what it was like to do battle with internal demons, and she wanted...needed to bring Connor into the light. "I'll be brave for both of us, Connor. Your new book is a beautiful tribute to Margo and Emmett. But they'd want your life to honor them as well."

"Shut up," he roared, whirling on her so violently that she stumbled back against the bed. "You don't know anything about Margo and Emmett. You and I have nothing." He swept out his arm, gesturing wildly. "This is nothing but make-believe."

"No." She whispered the word, not even certain if he could hear her with whatever noise was clattering through his head right now. "What we have is real. Those girls sleeping in the next room are real. You were here when they needed you. You found Shay."

He gave a sharp shake of his head. "Anyone could have—"

"But, more importantly, you saved Ranie."

"She wasn't lost."

"Yes, she was. In the same prison of sorrow that has you trapped. But you helped her. She trusts you. She needs you. You still have more to give, and I'm asking you to take a chance. Just try." She took a breath and then whispered, "Make the effort."

He grimaced and her instinct was to comfort him, to try to take away his pain despite the fact that her heart was shredded at his feet.

"I can't," he said, and walked out of the room.

It was as if he'd thrown her off a great cliff. At first there was only the sensation of falling, weightless and terrible. Then came the crash that shattered her until nothing was left but broken pieces.

April bent in front of the fireplace the next afternoon, carefully picking the pinecone figures out of the ash.

"I did that," Ranie said from behind her. "I'm sorry. I was mad about going to Aunt Tracy's and I threw them away."

Tapping the gray dust from the figure holding a yoga mat, April glanced over her shoulder and smiled. "It's a good thing we didn't light a fire last night."

The girl hesitated and then offered a tentative smile.

April turned and sat on the fireplace surround, patting the cool stone next to her. "What is it, sweetie?"

Slowly, Ranie lowered herself to sit, her hands clenched in fists on her thin legs. "What if you change your mind? I know I'm not all sunny and sweet like Shay, and I haven't been very nice to you. Are you sure you want me to stay, too?"

"Of course I am." April wrapped an arm around the girl's shoulders. "I'm not changing my mind, Ranie. Not now and not ever. No matter what happens."

"Are we the reason Connor left like he did?"

"What do you mean?"

"He didn't even say goodbye," she whispered.

"I'm sorry," April said, and pulled the girl closer. "He had an early flight and…" How could she make an excuse for something inexcusable? "I wish he would have handled it differently. He cared about you girls, but it's hard for him to admit that."

Ranie glanced up at April, her blue eyes unsure. "Sometimes Mom had boyfriends who wouldn't stick around once they found out about Shay and me. Back when Shay was a baby and Mom was healthy. She never said anything, but I could tell it made her sad. One of our neighbors would babysit and Mom would be so happy for a few weeks. Then she'd bring the guy around to meet us, and he'd be gone."

"I'm sorry. I'm sure your mom never blamed you. Those just weren't the right kind of men."

"But you really liked Connor and it makes you sad that he left."

April didn't bother to deny it. Even at twelve, Ranie could spot a lie without much effort. "I did like him, and I am sad."

"Me, too."

"But he didn't leave because of you and your sister." April took a deep breath and then added, "Or because of me. Some people are just too scared to let themselves be happy."

The girl nodded. "I was really angry when Mom died. I still am sometimes. I think about her and I hate that she's gone. I hate cancer. I hate being the girl with no mom. I wish I was like Shay, but I'm not."

"I understand," April admitted softly. "Sometimes I hate being defined by my breast cancer. I'm proud to be a survivor, but there is 'before cancer' and there is 'after cancer' and that will never change for either of us. All I ever want you to be is who you are. Even when you're mad or grumpy, I want you here. Even when I'm scared or unsure, I'm not giving you up. We're in this for the long haul. Do you understand?"

Tears shimmered in Ranie's eyes. "I want to be happy again," she whispered.

"Oh, sweetie." April hugged her tight. "You will. We will together." And because it was the right thing to do for this girl, April forced away her own heartache and let the love she felt for Ranie and Shay fill her heart. She wished it could have been different with Connor, and there was no denying that every part of her ached for him. But sadness and regret wouldn't rule her life. Her future was here in Crimson with these girls.

She shifted and turned toward the fireplace once more. "Let's rescue the rest of our pinecone family. I'm ready to head to our new home for the three of us."

"Where's Connor?"

April frowned. "Back in California by now, I imagine."

"No, I mean his pinecone." Ranie picked the two smaller figures out of the fireplace. "It's not here. Did you already throw it out?"

"I didn't touch it."

Ranie made a face and gave a creepy groan April would have expected to hear in a Halloween haunted house. "It's like he disappeared and was never really here in the first place."

April might believe that except for the deep ache in her heart. "We know he was here, and I believe that being with us this Christmas helped him. I hope he remembers us and it makes him feel a little better each time he does. He cared about you, Ranie. Don't ever doubt that."

"I know," the girl whispered. "It's hard to be happy after someone dies. I feel guilty sometimes when I smile or laugh, like I should always be missing Mom."

Thinking of how much emotional weight this girl carried on her shoulders made tears clog April's throat. "She'd want you to smile and laugh. You understand that, right?"

Ranie nodded, then stared at the two pinecone figures in her hand. "At first I felt bad that I liked you. I didn't want you to be nice because it felt like I was turning my back on my mom."

"I could never replace your mother, and I'd never try."

"I get that now," the girl answered, meeting April's gaze. "I'm happy we're going to be a family."

"Oh, sweetie, thank you." April hugged the girl tightly, so aware of the precious gift Jill had given to her. For someone who had thought she'd never have a family, the fact that for the rest of her life April would have the honor of caring for Ranie and Shay was tremendous. She sent up a silent prayer of thanks to her friend for entrusting her with these precious girls.

She gave the two pinecone figures Ranie held a pretend kiss with the one in her hand. "Let's find your sister and Jingle and head home."

Chapter Thirteen

"How is it possible that one person has so many mugs?" Sara Travers folded the lid on another cardboard box and taped the edges together.

It was New Year's Eve, and Sara, who had just returned from her vacation the previous day, had spent the whole morning helping April pack up her small apartment. Although the space had two bedrooms, April wanted a real house for the girls.

One great thing about the close-knit Crimson community was that people were willing to help out friends and neighbors. Her landlord had been the one to suggest the three-bedroom cottage only a few blocks from the elementary school. She'd quickly found someone to sublet her current rental so they'd be settled in their new home by the time school started next week.

"I like options for my tea," April said with a wink.

She stepped toward the window and looked down to where Ranie and Shay were making a snowman in the open space behind the building.

Sara came to stand beside her, wrapping an arm around April's waist. "I can't believe you didn't tell me about them when all of this started."

"It was temporary and I knew you'd—"

"Tell you to pull your head out of your butt and make a home for those girls?"

April laughed. "Pretty much. I thought I'd left my fear behind in California when we moved to Crimson."

"Yeah, right." Sara snorted. "Fear is like a barnacle. You have to scrape that sucker off with sandpaper."

"I don't think I've gotten rid of mine," April admitted. "I'm just learning to breathe through it."

"I like that plan." Sara stepped back and did an exaggerated mountain pose. "It's what makes you such a damn fine yoga teacher. You've got the Zen stuff down."

April turned to her. "You know, for the first time in as long as I can remember, I feel at peace. I still don't quite trust that I'm the best person for those girls, but I know I'm going to do my best to take care of them."

"Honey, you're the best person I know. You took care of me when I was a train wreck. If you can handle a washed-up Hollywood tabloid mess, you can handle Ranie and Shay." Sara put her hands on her hips and cocked a brow. "Speaking of hot messes, I heard you got quite chummy with Connor Pierce while he was here."

Absently, April pressed a hand to her chest. She'd gotten used to the ache that accompanied thoughts of

Connor, and now it felt almost like a companion. "It was kind of close quarters up at Cloud Cabin."

Sara leaned in. "Close as in 'between the sheets' close?"

April could feel heat rising to her cheeks and turned to the boxes stacked next to the bookshelf. "He let me read his manuscript. It was amazing."

"You slept with him," Sara whispered, her tone full of wonder. "You haven't gotten busy with a man since your divorce. That's a big deal, April."

"It wasn't." April was surprised how easily the lie rolled off her tongue. "We had a holiday fling. Nothing more."

"You don't do flings."

"I do," April said with a laugh that sounded hollow to her own ears. "When the guy runs away at the end."

"Oh, honey." Sara pulled her in for a tight hug. "Connor Pierce might be a brilliant author, but he's also a total idiot."

April sniffed and rested her head on her friend's shoulder. "I'm so glad you're back," she whispered with a sound that was somewhere between a laugh and a sob. "I'll be okay. The girls and I will make everything okay."

Sara stayed for lunch and then headed back to Crimson Ranch. She and Josh were hosting a big New Year's party later that night. April took the girls to buy school supplies and a few more clothes, since she wasn't sure when the boxes with the rest of their things that Jill's sister was shipping would arrive.

They played cards and then got ready for the party.

"Are all your friends nice?" Shay asked from the

backseat as April turned onto the dirt road that led to the ranch.

April glanced in the rearview mirror, thinking about how different this car ride was than that first day up the mountain. "They're all nice. You met most of them at the party at the bakery before Christmas."

Shay nodded, as if satisfied by the answer. "Will Brooke be there? She's going to be my friend at school. I like her."

Jake and Millie Travers's daughter, Brooke, was only a year older than Shay and April thought it was a good sign that Shay was excited to see her friend again.

"Yes, Brooke and her parents will be at the ranch tonight."

"I wish Connor was here," Ranie muttered, and then sucked in a breath, as if shocked she'd said the words out loud.

April wasn't surprised. She and Ranie had come a long way since their conversation at the cabin, but Connor was the one who'd been able to so easily smooth the girl's rough edges.

"What do you think he's doing for New Year's Eve?" Shay asked. This was a game the girl liked to play— what is Connor doing now? At different moments during the day, Shay would raise the question and then they'd all have to guess at the answer.

"I don't know, sweetie. Maybe he's going to a party with his friends."

"He can't be," Shay argued. "*We're* his friends."

"Who cares what he's doing?" Ranie snapped. "He left us, Shay."

"I know that," Shay answered softly. "Mommy left, too, but it doesn't stop me from loving either of them."

"Mom died." Ranie's tone was exasperated. "It's different."

"Have you girls ever seen fireworks above a mountain?" April made her tone bright, trying to push away the darkness of the heavy silence. "The town sets them off on the top of Crimson Mountain at midnight. The colors reflect off the snow and it's beautiful." She gave a small laugh as she parked the Jeep in the row of SUVs and trucks in front of the ranch's main house. "At least that's what I've heard. To tell you the truth, I've never been able to stay awake late enough to see them."

"Me and Brooke are going to be awake until the new year," Shay shouted. She bounced in her seat, the verbal sparring with her sister already forgotten. "I can stay up all night long."

April turned to see Ranie roll her eyes, but she was smiling at her sister. "We'll see about that, squirt."

Since she was an only child, Sara was the closest thing April had to a sister. She was getting used to the constant banter between the girls and the fact that she didn't have to mediate every exchange. Despite their differences in temperament, Ranie and Shay had a special bond and, once again, April felt a wash of gratitude that she'd been given the gift of caring for them.

They got out of the SUV, boots crunching in the snow as they approached the house. April could see people talking and laughing through the picture window, the bright warmth of the house's interior at odds with the bitterly cold night. A wistful sigh escaped her lips before she could stop it. Most of her friends in Crimson were half of a couple, and she suddenly realized that part of the reason she turned in early every

New Year's Eve was because she didn't have someone worth staying awake for to kiss at midnight.

It was time she opened herself to the possibility of finding love again. As much as she'd wanted it to be with Connor, there was no use pining for someone who couldn't love her back. A new year was a time for new beginnings, and she put dating on the list as her first resolution. The thought of being with anyone except Connor made the gaping void in her heart feel even more hollow.

Josh Travers greeted them at the door, and she was proud to introduce Shay and Ranie to him. They'd only taken a few steps into the house when Sara rushed forward and threw her arms around April.

"Nice to see you," April said, laughing at her friend's exuberance. "But you know it's only been a few hours since you were at the apartment."

"Don't be mad," Sara whispered in her ear. "Promise you won't be mad."

Before April could ask for an explanation, Shay's voice rang out in the now-silent room. "Connor's here!"

Everything disappeared except the man standing across the room, watching her from those piercing green eyes. His hair was shorter than it had been at Christmas, and the shadow of a beard covered his strong jaw. He wore a thick gray sweater and tan cargo pants with boots, and he looked rough and rugged, like he belonged in Colorado. In her world.

But she knew that was only an illusion, so her first instinct was to turn and flee. Then Ranie's hand slipped into hers. April forced herself to remain where she was as Shay ran forward, dodging other party guests to launch herself into Connor's arms.

April could feel the curious glances of her friends as he made his way toward her.

"Happy New Year," he said when he was standing only a few feet away.

"Connor," Shay said, practically bubbling over with excitement, "there's fireworks on the mountain at midnight. We're going to stay up and watch them."

"That's pretty late for a little girl," he answered, his voice gentle.

"April said I could." Shay wriggled in his arms and he lowered her to the ground. "And we're moving to a new house. Are you going to come see it? How long are you staying in Colorado?"

He smiled and tapped her on the nose. "That depends on my three favorite girls."

"You left," Ranie said softly, the two words at once a painful reminder and a condemnation, and exactly the sentiment April wanted to express.

"I'm sorry," he whispered, his gaze focusing on the girl. April tightened her grip on Ranie's hand, as if emotionally shoring up them both. "I was stupid."

"Truth," the girl muttered, and one side of Connor's mouth curved.

"I missed you, Ranie," he said. "There's no one to give me grief without you."

"Is that why you're here? Because email and text work a lot easier."

"I don't want email or texts. I want to be here. Now." He took a step toward the entry table and as he moved, his scent floated around April. Pine and spice—the combination almost brought her to her knees with the longing that poured through her. She tried to push her need back under the surface. "I also have something that belongs with you."

He picked up a gift box from the table and held it out to the girl. April curled her hand into a fist as Ranie released it to take the box. She opened it and let out a small gasp. "I knew you took it," she whispered. Lifting the pinecone figure holding a book out of the box, she turned toward April. "It didn't just disappear."

"No," April agreed, then fixed her gaze on the man now standing so close she could see the gold flecks around the edges of his eyes. "But you did. Why did you come back, Connor?"

"For you," he said without hesitation. "I came back for you."

Hope sliced through her fragmented defenses as she scrambled to shore up all the cracks in the walls that guarded her heart. She wasn't sure she could handle this moment without falling apart again.

She watched Shay tug on the hem of his sweater, her reaction to his return so simple. "I'm going to play with Brooke. Don't leave without saying goodbye, okay?"

"I'm not leaving," he told her, and with a nod, she skipped away. He met April's gaze again. "I'm not leaving," he repeated.

"My life isn't simple," she answered. "And I'm done making things easy for you." Behind Connor's shoulder, she saw Sara give her the thumbs-up and then Josh pulled his wife away. Suddenly it was all too much. Connor's return. Her friends watching. The way her heart stammered inside her chest.

She whirled around and made it several steps toward the front door before a hand grabbed her arm.

"April, don't run away."

"Don't you dare say that to me." She shrugged off his touch, grateful that at least since she'd moved into the foyer, all of her friends wouldn't bear witness to this. Whatever *this* turned out be. Her heart and her mind warred inside her head. "I'm not the one who ran. I pushed through my fears and doubts and I'm making life happen." She pointed at him, then lowered her hand when she realized her fingers were shaking. "You ran, Connor. When things got complicated, you took off."

"I'm sorry," he said again, and drew in a deep breath. "And you're right." He bent so that they were at eye level. "I'm scared to death, April. Every day. Every hour. Every minute and second. I can barely think for the fear pounding through me."

"I know." She bit down on her lip, hoping the small flicker of pain would stem the tide of her tears. She turned away again, her hand on the door.

"But it's nothing compared to the way I miss you." His voice hitched on the last word. She squeezed shut her eyes and didn't turn around.

Wouldn't turn. Because if she looked at him now, she was a goner. And as bad as the past few days had hurt, there wasn't enough left of her heart to keep going if he broke it again.

"Every moment I miss you," he said quietly. "Every time I take a breath, so I've actually done some experiments with holding my breath that would make David Blaine proud. It doesn't help. You are my breath. You are my heartbeat. You're my whole world, April."

She heard a broken sound and realized it had come from her.

"Turn around, sweetheart." His voice was gentle, coaxing. "Please turn around."

She did and the look in his eyes leveled her. It was open and real, and everything she'd wanted was right there in his gaze.

"I don't want to trust you," she whispered, because it was the truth and it was difficult, but she was finished being scared of either.

"Then just give me a chance to prove you can." His hand lifted before he pulled it back, running his fingers through his cropped hair. "The way you showed me that I deserve more than the half-life I was living. The way you proved to me that I can love again. I love you so damned much, April. Give me a chance. Give me forever."

She swallowed, but there was no stopping the tears now. They flowed hot and fast. She swiped at her cheeks. "I love you, too," she whispered.

His smile was tentative, hopeful. "I'm going to hold you now," he said, moving closer, crowding her against the door. "I'm going to hold you and never let you go."

Then he was wrapping her in his arms and she buried her face against his shoulder and cried. For what they'd both been through, what they'd lost and found and almost lost again. Everything in her heart poured out. The dam that had kept her emotions in check for so long simply burst under the force of her love. It was messy and real, and true to his word, Connor only held her tighter.

"Those are happy tears, right?"

April lifted her head as Connor shifted. Shay and Ranie stood in the doorway from the foyer to the family room, all the people she loved in the world watching behind them.

"The happiest," she whispered, and opened her

arms. Both girls ran forward and the four of them hugged. The joy April felt in this moment was so complete, nothing could compare. Nothing except the peace that descended a few moments later. Because she'd finally found her family, and she was never letting them go.

Epilogue

Six Months Later

Connor looked up from the podium as he finished his reading and the crowd gathered in the San Francisco bookstore started to clap. He took a deep breath, only exhaling when his gaze found April and the girls standing at the back of the room.

She smiled, and both Ranie and Shay waved. Because it was summer break, they'd been able to join him in several of the six cities on his current book tour. Of course, after the first two readings Shay had decided that his book was too "growned up" for her taste, and the three of them usually arrived at the end of each appearance. Every single time, seeing them made his heart expand with love and gratitude.

He owed April more than he could ever repay. She'd

brought him back to life and given him the second chance he hadn't realized he'd so desperately needed.

The bookstore manager allowed a few minutes of questions from the audience before leading Connor to the table stacked with his books. He signed copies and spoke with fans for almost an hour before the event was over.

April and the girls were waiting for him in the tiny coffee bar next to the store's main entrance.

"We got ice cream," Shay announced, holding up a half-eaten cone. "But April said we still have to eat dinner at the party."

"Since you're growing like a weed," he said, nipping at the ice cream, "I'm sure it won't be a problem."

"Unless they serve brussels sprouts," she told him. "Those are yucky."

"Hey," April protested with a smile. "I roasted brussels sprouts last week. They were delicious."

"Whatever you say." Shay licked at her ice cream.

"Margo's mother is a wonderful cook," he told the girl, slipping into the chair between her and April. "She'll have something there you'll like."

"And you're sure they're okay with all of us coming to the party?" Ranie's blue eyes were filled with worry. "It's not going to be weird?"

"It might be weird at first," Connor admitted. They had a hotel room downtown but were driving out to the suburbs to have dinner with Margo's family and a few of Connor and Margo's mutual friends. He'd slowly gotten back in touch with the people who had loved his wife, bolstered by April's support and encouragement. He'd found that, instead of sorrow and guilt, sharing memories of Margo and Emmett now triggered a quiet peace. That peace strengthened the love he felt for the family he'd lost, but also allowed him to move forward with the family he was creating with April and the girls. "The Malones are really nice and they love kids." He leaned over the table. "Just don't pick your nose at the table."

She snorted. "I don't pick my nose."

He flashed her a grin. "Then you should be fine."

"You had a lot of super fans in the audience tonight," April said, reaching for his hand. "Everyone was excited to meet the famous author."

"Not as excited as the author was to get back to his wife," he whispered, and lifted her fingers to his mouth, gently kissing the diamond band on her left hand. They'd married in a small service a week into the new year. It had been a whirlwind, but Connor had no doubt he wanted to spend the rest of his life with April at his side. They'd agreed that it was important for the girls that they get married before he relocated to Colorado to move in with them.

With Ranie and Shay as witnesses, they'd had a ceremony at Cloud Cabin. He'd joined them in their rental house, but they'd recently purchased an acre of land outside of town to build their dream home. April's friends had quickly become his friends, and living in the shadow of the rugged beauty of Crimson Mountain was just one more thing that added to his healing.

"Can I go look at books?" Ranie asked.

"Me, too," Shay shouted around her last bite of ice-cream cone, jumping up from her chair.

"Yes, but stay together," April told them with a gentle smile. "And don't plan on buying anything more.

We're going to need a whole room in the new house for the books you've collected on every stop of this trip."

Both girls looked at Connor.

He glanced at April out of the corner of his eye. "How can you say no to books?"

"You're totally throwing me under the bus," she said with a laugh.

"I'm not," he protested, drawing her closer and kissing the top of her head. "But we're talking about books," he whispered into her hair.

"One book each," she told the girls with a sigh.

They fist bumped and then headed for the children's section.

She pulled back, her dark eyes gentle. "How are you feeling about tonight?"

"Nervous but positive," he admitted. "When I spoke with Margo's mother earlier, she was excited about meeting you and the girls. I think the guilt and blame I carried was a burden for more than just me. They really were my family, and somehow it helps their healing to know that I'm moving forward." He leaned in for a kiss. "But I'm happy that this is the last stop on the book tour."

She smiled against his mouth. "We're going home."

Home.

The word that had left him hollow for so long now filled him with a happiness he hadn't believed possible.

"You are my home," he whispered, cupping her face between his palms. "I love you, April. I'll love you forever."

"I love you, too, Connor. Forever."

Connor understood that life held no guarantees, but through the darkness and light, with April at his side he would appreciate each step on the journey. He'd never again take for granted the peace that filled his soul, and he intended to spend every day proving his love to April and the girls.

* * * * *

Be sure to catch Michelle Major's next book,
A FORTUNE IN WAITING,
the first book in
THE FORTUNES OF TEXAS:
THE SECRET FORTUNES *continuity,*
coming in January 2017!

And don't miss the previous installments in the
CRIMSON, COLORADO *miniseries:*

ALWAYS THE BEST MAN
A BABY AND A BETROTHAL
A VERY CRIMSON CHRISTMAS
SUDDENLY A FATHER
A SECOND CHANCE AT CRIMSON RANCH
A KISS ON CRIMSON RANCH

available now wherever Harlequin Special Edition
books and ebooks are sold.

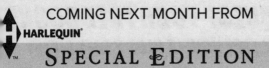

COMING NEXT MONTH FROM

HARLEQUIN®

SPECIAL EDITION

Available December 20, 2016

#2521 A FORTUNE IN WAITING
The Fortunes of Texas: The Secret Fortunes • by Michelle Major
Everyone in Austin is charmed by architect Keaton Fortune Whitfield, the sexy new British Fortune in town—except Francesca Harriman, waitress at Lola May's and the one woman he wants in his life! Can he win the heart of the beautiful hometown girl?

#2522 TWICE A HERO, ALWAYS HER MAN
Matchmaking Mamas • by Marie Ferrarella
When popular news reporter Elliana King interviews Colin Benteen, a local police detective, she had no idea this was the man who tried to save her late husband's life—nor did she realize that he would capture her heart.

#2523 THE COWBOY'S RUNAWAY BRIDE
Celebration, TX • by Nancy Robards Thompson
Lady Chelsea Ashford Alden was forced to flee London after her fiancé betrayed her, and now seeks refuge with her best friend in Celebration. When Ethan Campbell catches her climbing in through a window, he doesn't realize the only thing Chelsea will be stealing is his heart...

#2524 THE MAKEOVER PRESCRIPTION
Sugar Falls, Idaho • by Christy Jeffries
Baseball legend Kane Chatterson has tried hard to fly under the radar since his epic scandal—until a beautiful society doctor named Julia Fitzgerald comes along and throws him a curveball! She may be a genius, but men were never her strong suit. Who better than the former MVP of the dating scene to help her out?

#2525 WINNING THE NANNY'S HEART
The Barlow Brothers • by Shirley Jump
When desperate widower Sam Millwright hires Katie Williams to be his nanny, he finds a way back to his kids—and a second chance at love.

#2526 HIS BALLERINA BRIDE
Drake Diamonds • by Teri Wilson
Former ballerina and current jewelry designer Ophelia Rose has caught the eye of the new CEO of Drake Diamonds, Artem Drake, but she has more secrets than the average woman. A kitten, the ballet and *lots* of diamonds might just help these two lonely souls come together in glitzy, snowy New York City.

**YOU CAN FIND MORE INFORMATION ON UPCOMING HARLEQUIN® TITLES,
FREE EXCERPTS AND MORE AT WWW.HARLEQUIN.COM.**

HSECNM1216

"The dog wasn't the silver lining." He tapped one finger on the top of the box. "You and pie are the silver lining. I hope you have time to have a piece with me." He leaned in. "You know it's bad luck to eat pie alone."

She made a sound that was half laugh and half sigh. "That might explain some of the luck I've had in life. I hate to admit the amount of pie I've eaten on my own."

His heart twisted as a pain she couldn't quite hide flared in those caramel eyes. His well-honed protective streak kicked in, but it was also more than that. He wanted to take up the sword and go to battle against whatever dragons had hurt this lovely, vibrant woman.

It was an idiotic notion, both because Francesca had never given him any indication that she needed assistance slaying dragons and because he didn't have the genetic makeup of a hero. Not with Gerald Robinson as his father.

But he couldn't quite make himself walk away from the chance to give her what he could that might once again put a smile on her beautiful face.

"Then it's time for a dose of good luck." He stepped back and pulled out a chair at the small, scuffed conference table in the center of the office. "I can't think of a better way to begin than with a slice of Pick-Me-Up Pecan Pie. Join me?"

Her gaze darted to the door before settling on him. "Yes, thank you," she murmured and dropped into the seat.

Her scent drifted up to him—vanilla and spice, perfect for the type of woman who would bake a pie from scratch. He'd never considered baking to be a particularly sexy activity, but the thought of Francesca wearing an apron in the kitchen as she mixed ingredients for his pie made sparks dance across his skin.

The mental image changed to Francesca wearing nothing but an apron and—

"I have plates," he shouted and she jerked back in the chair.

"That's helpful," she answered quietly, giving him a curious look. "Do you have forks, too?"

"Yes, forks." He turned toward the small bank of cabinets installed in one corner of the trailer. "And napkins," he called over his shoulder. Damn, he sounded like a complete prat.

Don't miss
A FORTUNE IN WAITING by Michelle Major,
available January 2017 wherever
Harlequin® Special Edition books and ebooks are sold.

www.Harlequin.com